THE DOOR TO DOOR POET

My Adventures Across England

Rowan McCabe

Published in 2025
by Eye Books Ltd
29A Barrow Street
Much Wenlock
Shropshire
TF13 6EN
www.eye-books.com

ISBN: 9781785634345

Copyright © Rowan McCabe 2025
Cover by Mark Mecob

Typeset in Bembo Std and TT Norms

British Library Cataloguing in Publication Data
A catalogue record for this book is available from the British Library

Our authorised representative in the EU for product safety is:
Logos Europe, 9 rue Nicolas Poussin, 17000, La Rochelle, France
contact@logoseurope.eu

For Rose, my mam and Stephen

Most people ignore most poetry
because most poetry ignores most people
Adrian Mitchell

You don't want to try that round here
A resident, Stockton-on-Tees

CONTENTS

PROLOGUE

I WAS STANDING IN THE KITCHEN while Rose chopped a tomato.

'And you'll only be an hour?' she asked.

I told her I would only be an hour at the most.

'And you promise you won't go inside anyone's house? Even if they invite you in?'

I promised.

'Are you sure this is a good idea, Rowan?'

'I'm sure,' I said, after hesitating for a little longer than I'd have liked. 'I mean, I think so. It can't be that bad, can it? What's the worst that could happen?'

She looked really worried then. Which was fair enough. On reflection, there were probably quite a lot of bad things that could happen. But it was best not to think about those. At least not right now, anyway.

I left the kitchen and went into the bedroom. I paced left, then right. I took some deep breaths. I started to practise what I was going to say. Then the phone rang. It was Matt.

'I've got a gig near your house today. Do you want to

come?'

I told him I couldn't. I explained why.

He sounded confused.

'Are you sure this is a good idea, Rowan?'

It was a response I was beginning to get used to.

A week before this, I'd met up with my friend Scott in a pub called the Cumberland Arms. As we sipped on our pints, I outlined the general plan.

'In Newcastle?' he gasped, before laughing – for ages and ages.

It wasn't a cruel laugh. It was a laugh of genuine disbelief. The way you might laugh at a goat trying to fill in a tax return.

In his defence, I could see the funny side.

This was easily the stupidest idea I'd ever had. But I'd told loads of people I was going to do it now. I was already in too deep. This afternoon, I was going to knock on some strangers' doors and offer to write a poem for them.

I went back to thinking about what I was going to say. It felt like, if I introduced myself as a poet, anyone who answered would slam the door in my face. Maybe I could tell them I was doing an art project? That seemed a bit more relatable. Yes, that was it. I'd tell them I was doing an art project and then I'd launch into the introductory poem. No explanation, no preamble.

I messed with my hair a bit. I tried to appear less manic. I felt even more nervous than I did before. I was worried about the way this might affect things. At best, it was going to seem like I was up to no good. At worst, I was going to seem kind of…vulnerable.

Despite my assurances to Rose, the reality of the situation was beginning to weigh on me. What exactly was the worst thing that could happen here? A punch in the face? *Worse?*

I couldn't believe I'd put myself up for this. I felt terrified. But it was too late to go back. In precisely four minutes, I was going to step out into that street and attempt Door-to-Door Poetry for the first time.

This is the story of what happened.

Introductory Poem

I'm a Door-to-Door Poet
and I know that sounds quite crazy,
but this could be worse though,
I could be the Avon lady.

In school they taught me poetry's bust,
wrote by toffs who've turned to dust
on country manors, deathly shrouds,
serious lords and fluffy clouds.

I found it quite hard to relate,
I grew up on a rough estate,
walls thin as paper used to trace,
the clouds an endless tone of grey.

I'm here to make poetry exciting,
like bungee jumping, but less frightening,
and I'm standing here to find
the subjects that flow through your mind.

Tell me about your life.
OK, maybe not the whole of it.
I'll stick it in a poem
or at least have a decent go at it.

Maybe you heard a great story
you'd love to see in rhyme.
Maybe your blood is boiling
from a recent council fine.

Maybe you dropped your smart phone
and it fell down the toilet,
I don't know – I can't decide for you
'cos that would spoil it.

So cheers for listening to these verses,
I hope I got across my purpose,
don't slam the door, don't be nervous,
the Door-to-Door Poet is at your service.

Dear Cheryl,

It's with very mixed emotions that I have to inform you of my resignation from Butterflies and Bugs, with immediate effect, on 14/01/19. It's been an absolute pleasure working at the after-school club for more than 5 years and my decision is by no means a reflection on the staff, young people, or the quality of the job. I am, however, off to be a full-time poet, and will need to spend every hour of the day stroking my chin, gazing at clouds and weeping openly beneath oak trees. Please send my well wishes to everyone at the club, I'll miss them a lot.

Kind regards,

Rowan McCabe

From: ████████████

Sent: Tuesday, January 15, 2019, 10:36 AM

To: Rowan McCabe

Subject: Re: Resignation

Thank you Rowan

I love this email. Hilarious but really lovely at the same time. I'll pass on your well wishes.

Many Thanks

Cheryl ████████████

1

BEGINNINGS

IT'S BEEN SAID THAT LIFE is what happens while you're making other plans. By that logic, if you have no plans at all, does that mean you're living life to the fullest? Or does it mean that you are dead?

If I tried to draw a picture of a life well lived, I don't think it would include someone sitting on a sofa eating a gateau in their underpants at 11am. And, even if that really is the best use of a human life, what are you supposed to talk to the guy in the corner shop about?

These were just some of the questions running through my mind in the weeks building up to my Door-to-Door Poetry adventure, in a time when everything seemed a lot more normal.

It all started when I quit my job.

For the past five years I'd been working in an after-school club. My official job description was to 'facilitate good play' which, in practice, had mostly involved handing out Sellotape and making sure nobody ran with scissors.

It was a nice place. I got on with the other staff. But something wasn't quite right. Pretty soon I would be thirty.

I had recently purchased an ironing board. I was coming to feel like, as much as I didn't mind it, working in the after-school club wasn't exactly what I'd imagined I'd be doing for the rest of my days.

At the start of the new year, I'd decided I was going to quit. I didn't really know what I was going to do after that. I was hoping that leaving would give me a bit of space to figure it out. In reality, this had mostly involved staring aimlessly out of the window and eating my own body weight in muffins.

You might say I was finding it a little hard to adjust. Before I'd worked at the after-school club, I'd been in a call centre. Before that, I was an English Literature student. For the first time I could really remember, I didn't have anywhere to be.

You may have found yourself in a similar situation. It's the kind of thing that sounds great on paper. But, like reading a childhood diary, or watching an episode of *Love Island*, when it comes down to it, it can actually be quite unsettling.

So much of our identity is bound up with this idea of what we 'do', isn't it? It's one of the first questions we ask someone when we meet them. One thing I'd enjoyed about being a student was the way it had answered that question succinctly and avoided any further probing.

It doesn't matter if you have no idea what makes you happy. It doesn't matter if your kitchen is piled high with dirty dishes, or if you've stopped using your front door for fear of persistent bailiffs. If someone asks what you do and you say 'I'm a student', that is enough. You have passed society's test. You are an official, functioning human being.

Even though I wasn't happy at the after-school club, similar rules had applied there too.

No one had asked me what I did since I'd quit, but I knew that question would be coming sooner or later. I had a feeling telling them 'Nothing' wasn't going to go down in quite the same way.

I was living in a one-bedroom flat with my girlfriend, Rose. We'd met during the second year of our degree.

I first spoke to Rose outside one of the lecture halls. I knew she liked books already, and I'd been scribbling away at poems and sharing them at open mic nights. So, in a fit of overconfidence, I'd asked her to come along to a reading I was doing at an event called 'Pints and Poetry', which very much did what it said on the tin.

Amazingly, she said yes. Perhaps even more amazingly, she agreed to keep seeing me afterwards. In the summer months, we'd go for picnics in the park and I'd pretend to understand Keats in a desperate attempt to impress her. Before too long, we were officially an item.

I remember how sophisticated I felt when we got the keys to our place. Gone were my days of being a greasy bachelor. No more would I trip over ash-filled cans to get to a toilet covered in sick. I was going to live in a real house. With my girlfriend. We would have an assortment of cushions. We would drink wine out of actual glasses.

There was a desk in the living room. Dark brown wood; aluminium legs. And it was here that I found myself, swinging backwards and forwards on the rickety second-hand office chair, when I realised there was no start time, no deadlines, no obligations. Rose set off for work to her teaching job and I was left on my own, the day stretching out before me in all its intimidating wonder.

Clearly, I needed some kind of a focus. I needed a project in which to invest my time and to realise my potential. I'd decided that I wanted it to have something to do with poetry. I'd been writing for a few years now. I'd appeared at a lot more open mic nights. I'd even taken part in the occasional street performance. The trouble was, as anyone who's ever tried will tell you, poetry, like Morris dancing, or playing the penny whistle, is an incredibly niche and difficult field to make a living in.

I might as well face it, I thought. Poetry was never going be a proper job. It's not like you'd ever have to clock in and do a nine-to-five.

But imagine if you did… Imagine if you had to go around knocking on doors. Like a charity fundraiser. Or a door-to-door salesman.

Somewhere in the back of my muffin-dazed mind, I'd begun to design a little project for myself. This would turn out to be quite a pivotal moment in my life, something that would give me a newfound sense of meaning and purpose. But it had started off as a bit of a joke: *what if you knocked on a stranger's door and offered to write them a poem?*

My first thoughts were that, surely, someone had tried something like this before.

I googled it. There was nothing. Just a few cryptic poems

about doors.

The more I thought about it, the more I was seriously beginning to plan how this might actually work.

I decided early on that, if I really was going to try this, I wasn't going to ask for any money. It seemed like you'd only meet people who already liked poetry that way, and the odds of finding them were slim-to-none.

Still, from my experiences on stages and street corners over the years, I'd come to believe that some people might enjoy the stuff a bit more than they first thought. Every now and again, I'd been approached by an audience member who had sheepishly introduced themselves, before confessing something that had given my life an unprecedented level of direction: 'Excuse me. I don't really like poetry, but I quite enjoyed that.'

Surely it couldn't hurt to try, could it ?

The time for deliberating, it seemed, was over. If I set a deadline, I knew it would make it all feel a bit more real. I decided I would do it on a Saturday, to give people the best chance of being off work. I'd try around midday, so I could still have a lie-in. I wrote a poem to introduce myself. I memorised it, then timed myself saying it out loud. It was a minute and ten seconds long.

I felt like I needed to think of something different to wear too. A costume. Something mock-formal. I knew Rose would be able to help. It also seemed like I should probably tell her where I was going, just in case anything went wrong.

After talking her down from the ceiling, and assuring her

I would only be gone for an hour or so, she agreed to get involved, so long as I promised to carry a mobile phone at all times and didn't accept any sweets from strangers.

We got a black overcoat from a charity shop. She found me a brown leather briefcase at a local flea market.

It was dusty and scuffed and it had a hole in the side, but it's hard to adequately describe the power of that briefcase. It had a transformative effect on me. Like Excalibur. It was only when I held it in my hands that I felt like a real, bona fide Door-to-Door Poet.

The evening before the big day, I did what I always do when I feel like I'm on the verge of something potentially life-changing: I went out for a curry. There are few things in this world that are sweeter or more satisfying than a well-made vegetable dhansak. I should have been completely and utterly content.

But that night, as I lay in bed, my stomach was churning. I don't think it was on account of the dhansak. My thoughts kept wandering to tomorrow, to the challenge ahead.

What was the worst thing that could actually happen here? A punch in the face? *Worse?* No matter how much I tried to ignore it, the question kept coming back.

I wasn't sure what the answer was yet. But I'd decided I was going to find out.

Out There

Somewhere, across the street,
life is really happening.
The sun is dawning, people
awake well-rested,
unafraid to face the day.

A woman arranges her
breakfast into the face of
a favourite newscaster.
A man walks the dog,
appreciating the shape
of ancient chimney tops.

Strangers make time to
mark important dates,
to savour each taste.
Nobody feels ashamed
of lessons learned the hard way.

Somewhere, across the street,
life is really happening.
So I tap against the pane,
scrape at the surface and try,
but on this dark January evening,
it is difficult to find.

2

HEATON

I STEPPED OUT OF THE HOUSE on the 2nd of February 2019. My heart racing, my legs like jelly. Not long before this, Greggs the bakers had launched its first ever vegan sausage roll.

It was a move that had led to great controversy. Opinions on the matter were deeply divided. If people could be this angry about the existence of a vegan sausage roll, what kind of impact might I have on the general public's psyche?

I hadn't really considered which house I was going to start at. I'd imagined it would be somewhere on my street. As soon as my foot hit the pavement, however, I knew there was absolutely no way I could knock on any of the doors here.

They were just too close. What if it all went tits up? What if I made a fool of myself? I was going to have to see that person on a pretty regular basis. The trip to the corner shop is stressful enough as it is.

I decided to try a street nearby instead – somewhere close, so that they were still my neighbour, but far enough away that, in the worst-case scenario, I could just avoid that spot for the rest of my life.

I knew it wouldn't be too difficult. This part of Newcastle is a dense grid of Victorian terraces. There's a long road called Second Avenue and cutting across it are various other streets – Fifth Avenue, Sixth Avenue, etc.

Despite the crippling nerves, I was also feeling kind of relieved. I'd spent so many weeks worrying about what might happen. It struck me that, whatever the actual outcome, in a few minutes I'd finally know the answer.

This, at least in theory, was how Door-to-Door Poetry was going to work:

1) Knock on a door and count to forty-five in my head.
2) When someone answers, do the poem that asks them what is important to them.
3) Have a conversation about it.
4) Take out a form and record the person's name and address, then arrange a date and a time for the delivery.

The plan was to head back a few weeks later with the finished poem in hand, to read it out on the doorstep for every person. Though at this point, I had no idea if I would actually get that far.

I started walking down Second Avenue. I spotted a sign for Mundella Terrace. This seemed good. It was nearby. Also, Mundella sounds a bit like Mandela, doesn't it? Nelson Mandela was a nice guy. Maybe the people on this street would be nice too.

I crossed the road onto a long row of red-brick terraces.

Everything around me looked a shade darker. A couple walked past on the pavement and it felt like they were staring at me. It felt like the whole world was staring at me.

I walked to the top of the street and found myself standing outside a house with a green door and an empty concrete yard, running over what I was going to say again and again in my head. I took a deep breath, opened the gate and walked up the path. I knocked on the door. A knock that I hoped would sound both jovial and casual.

I paused.

What was that?

A shuffling sound. The nerves were unbearable now. It felt like the floor was sinking, like I was in a lift. I was just standing there, staring at the little spyhole in the door. Was somebody looking through it? Checking me out to see if I was a murderer? OK, note to self: try as hard as you can not to look like a murderer.

I realised I was dressed a lot like a door-to-door salesman. It had seemed really funny and tongue-in-cheek at the time, but that was what they were going to think I was, wasn't it? I considered shouting: 'It's OK, I'm a poet!'

No. I needed to move on.

But what if I didn't wait long enough? What if someone came out at the next door, and I started talking to them, and then the first person came out after that? *OK, I'll just count,* I thought. *I'll just count to a certain number and then move on.* But how long is long enough in a situation like this? Forty-five seconds? It takes me much longer than forty-five seconds to answer the door sometimes. Should I count for another forty-five? Is this what a delivery driver has to think about every time they knock? I was never going to be angry about a delivery driver not waiting long enough again.

I headed back onto the pavement. I stepped through the next gate and walked up the path. I rang the bell.

Someone was coming! *JESUS – THIS WAS IT!*

The bolts were clicking, the door was opening, my heart was pounding around in my chest like it was in a washing machine.

A girl was standing there in her early twenties. Black hair, chestnut eyes.

'Excuse me, my name is Rowan and I'm doing an art project. I don't want any money or anything. I was just wondering if you had a minute and ten seconds to spare and I could tell you a bit more about it?'

'Yeah, OK.'

She said yes! I launched into my introductory poem, trying very hard not to forget the words.

'I'm a Door-to-Door Poet, and I know that sounds quite crazy, but…'

She looked a little unsure. I don't think she could tell it was a poem. She was nodding and saying 'alright'. A lot. Like it was a normal conversation. This was weird. I felt like The Cat in the Hat. I was talking in rhyme and she was answering, but she was not answering in rhyme.

I got to the end.

'So basically,' I told her, 'I'm going door-to-door writing poems for strangers on any subject that's important to them and I wondered if I could write one for you.'

She looked worried now, her features wrinkling up like a crisp packet on a teenage bonfire.

'Erm, I don't know.' She *sounded* worried too. 'I like shopping. I like…er…friends.'

I considered writing a poem about two of the blandest subjects imaginable.

'You know what? I've got some bacon on in the kitchen. I'm sorry.'

No.

It wasn't supposed to be like this. The hardest part I could imagine was trying to persuade someone to listen. I hadn't really considered the idea that they might listen and still not want to get involved.

I stepped back onto the pavement. I tried a few more doors. There were a few no answers. The street was deadly silent. It occurred to me that it was a Saturday, that there was a match on. Everyone was probably out enjoying themselves, weren't they? Like normal people. What the hell was I doing with my life?

A little further down the road, two lads answered with beanie hats on. They looked spaced out and confused – a bit like I do when I answer the door. I remembered it was mushroom season. Man, this would really mess with your head if you were on mushrooms, wouldn't it?

'Sorry mate,' said one of them, in slow motion. 'We're just on our way out. Have you got a flyer for it?'

'No. It's pretty early stages actually,' I replied. As in, I need you to tell me what to write about, or it will never get off the ground.

A few more houses, a few no answers. And then, towards the end of the street, I got to a blue door with a silver knocker. A lad in his twenties came out in a vest and shorts. He looked a bit like Brad Pitt. When he said hello, he sounded a bit like Brad Pitt too, if Brad Pitt was from Yorkshire.

I asked him if he had a minute. He told me he did. I started doing the poem. HE WAS LAUGHING! Oh my god, I couldn't believe it! He was laughing. He was actually enjoying it! I was doing a poem for him and he was enjoying it.

'You know what?' he said. 'You're the first poet I've ever met.' He told me his name was Kyle.

'Well, Kyle,' I said, shaking his hand heartily, 'I know a lot of people don't think poetry is very relevant to their lives. So I'm going door-to-door writing poems for people on any subject they like. Tell me, what's important to you? What are your interests?'

The Story of the Surfing Yorkshireman

The brochures boast of endless sun,
of waves that break like Hokusai's.
A paradise for anyone
whose surfboard skills are highly prized.
In the sea, porpoises come
to squeak and frolic in the fun
but somewhere, sulking near the harbour,
a surfing Yorkshireman hates Scarborough.

He sits on one bench, constantly,
wet-suited, surfboard by his side.
But on the beach he won't be seen,
even in the highest tide.
He sighs and glares back at the sea
like it's his lifelong enemy.
And if you passed him, you might spy
the teardrops running from his eye.

But why, Yorkshireman? Why so sad?
Can you not see the town's great beauty?
How could your very soul withstand
its charmed Victorian majesty?
The castle, sprinkled on the crags,
is its wonder not your bag?
Have you tried the dodgems at the bay?
The Yorkshireman just turns away.

He answers: *No, none of the bricks*
of this town broke me down to tears.
The surfing here is proper shit,
I haven't seen a wave in years.
The water's calm and full of grit,
it's yellow as a blue whale's piss.
O pray, what could survive out there
in that dead ocean of despair?

But why don't you just drive away,
Yorkshireman? I'm so confused.
Go to Cornwall, or Whitley Bay,
even for an afternoon?
With torment in his voice, he says
I can never leave this place!
For I'm the cursed and lonely creature
who is the local surfing teacher.

3

BOSTON ARRIVAL

THE MOMENT I HAD THE IDEA for Door-to-Door Poetry, I was walking down the street I live on. It's a pretty normal row of terraces, there's about 300 people living around me. For the first time in my life, I realised I didn't know any of them.

I don't think that's particularly unusual, is it? A lot of people don't talk to their neighbours. But until this point, I'd never really noticed how odd that was.

My conversation with Kyle had been brief, but it had given me a glimpse of an exciting new frontier. I was now an official Door-to-Door Poet.

I went back to deliver Kyle's poem a few weeks later. The plan was to read it out to him in person, then give him a written copy. But as I walked along Mundella Terrace that day, I found myself worrying about whether Kyle would be in when I arrived.

There were other potential complications I hadn't really considered. What if Kyle was in, but it wasn't a good time to talk? What if he felt obliged to listen to me reading the poem when he was actually in the middle of something much more important?

It would have been great if I could have phoned ahead first. But I hadn't thought to take his number. I didn't even know his second name. When it came down to it, the sheer thrill of finding someone had completely taken over.

In the end, I needn't have been worried. I tapped Kyle's knocker and he answered pretty much immediately, wearing a bright blue pair of Hawaiian shorts.

'How do?' he asked.

I said hello. I explained that I'd come to deliver his poem.

'Well, you best come in then,' he said.

I followed Kyle through the door and we took a left into the living room. I sat down on a dark green armchair and pulled the poem out of my briefcase. Kyle perched on a sofa nearby and I started to read it to him.

It felt a bit strange. I was used to doing this kind of thing on stages, where you can look around the room.

But this was a poem written for one person. In their house. It was difficult to know how much to look at Kyle while I read it. Making too much eye contact seemed a bit intense. But not looking at him at all felt kind of antisocial. I made a conscious effort to aim for somewhere in the middle.

I wasn't sure what Kyle was making of it all. I could see there was a pressure on him too, to look like he was enjoying it. To pull his 'I'm enjoying having a poem read to me' face.

By the end of it, Kyle settled for a very Yorkshire: 'That were good, that,' before shaking my hand and patting me on the shoulder.

He told me the poem felt well-timed. He'd been out for

a surf only just the other day. He said he didn't dislike his home town quite as much as I'd made out, but he'd enjoyed hearing what I'd written all the same.

It felt good to get to know someone who lived near me a little bit better, to feel more connected to the place I lived in. And I found it interesting that, whenever I walked down Kyle's street after this, it didn't seem quite as imposing as it had before.

Of course, it could have all ended right there, on Kyle's doorstep. That could have been my first and only outing as a Door-to-Door Poet. But I'm pleased to say that it wasn't. And, after my meeting with Kyle, I'd started planning something very big and very silly.

But before I tell you what that was, we're going to need to go back a bit. We need to get to know each other a little better first.

Let's start with the basics.

My name is Rowan. I live in Newcastle upon Tyne and, as you already know, I write poetry.

I'm going to be subjecting you to quite a bit of that in the following pages. So before we go any further, I want to make something absolutely, abundantly clear: I've always found it a bit weird describing myself as a poet. I know what most people think of when they hear that word. It conjures up images of frilly shirts and lying in meadows in a deep malaise.

And if you think liking poetry makes you a bit odd, try liking poetry in a post-industrial town in the north-east of England. The McCabes have always done very manual jobs.

My grandparents were miners and shipbuilders.

Don't get me wrong – my family have always been really supportive. But when I told them I wanted to be a poet, for a living, it was a bit like announcing that I wanted to become a wizard. From that point forward they stared back at me with a mixture of confusion, and what I interpreted as a form of pity.

Not long after my first outing as a Door-to-Door Poet, I'd been on a passing trip to Edinburgh. It was there that I'd had a very important conversation, one which was to turn everything that had happened so far on its head.

I'd popped into what is supposedly the city's 'Most Haunted Pub'. Over a glass of their finest pale, I'd got chatting to a very well-spoken lady at the bar, whose name I never asked, but who I now like to assume was called Cathy. Cathy told me she was visiting from London. Our conversation had turned to how I'd been filling my time.

I'd told Cathy that trying Door-to-Door Poetry had felt like an experiment. An experiment in kindness. It was an experiment that had, so far at least, really restored my faith in humanity. It had left me with the feeling that people are, generally, pretty decent. That strangers will stop to help you if you approach them in the right way.

The woman had replied enthusiastically. Perhaps a little too enthusiastically.

'This is such a fun idea,' she smiled. 'But it would only ever work in the North-East.'

And, with that, my life changed direction forever.

It didn't happen right away, of course. These things rarely

do.

A little defensively, I'd told Cathy I disagreed. Of course it would work in other places. I reckoned you could try Door-to-Door Poetry absolutely anywhere. I just so happened to have tried it in Newcastle because that's where I live. Case closed. End of story.

But like the slow dripping of a leaky tap, the statement of this metropolitan stranger had come back to my mind in choice moments of quiet solitude, with a regularity and persistence that could no longer be ignored.

You see, the more I thought about Cathy's comment, the more it revealed an awkward truth. If I was being really honest with her and, ultimately, with myself, I had to admit that I didn't actually know the answer. I had absolutely no idea. I knew nothing at all about the rest of the country, or the people who were living in it.

It's not that I don't travel. It's just that my choice of destination is usually a bit further afield. Places where the sun is hotter, the beer cheaper.

But even that doesn't really get to the heart of the problem. Because the fact of the matter is that I am, and always have been, absolutely crap at geography. I am, if you will, 'geographically challenged'. I once tried to argue, for much longer than I'd care to admit, that Shakespeare came from Milton Keynes. My understanding of the country I live in ended somewhere just above Bedlington and just below Sunderland. And even though I'd travelled to other places in England before, I'd never really been paying much attention to where I was going, or what the make-up of the town was like when I'd arrived.

It wasn't long before Cathy's statement was plaguing my every waking moment. I couldn't stop thinking about it. She'd said that Geordies and people from Scarborough are, and I quote, 'exceptionally kind'. She'd said that there was absolutely no way this would work down South. Ever. And as much as I wanted to disagree with her, I could see her point.

Geordies, like most people in the North-East, are renowned for being friendly. It's part of our USP. It goes hand in hand with the ability to brave sub-zero temperatures with no coat and an excessive consumption of alcohol on any and every social occasion.

Was my conversation with Kyle some kind of fluke? Some accident of locality? What if strangers weren't really as kind as I thought they were?

I needed to know the answer. And I'd come up with a way of finding out for sure.

It was now April 2019 and I had just set off on an adventure.

It was an adventure that was to take me a bit further afield than my immediate neighbourhood – 11,617 miles, to be exact. By train, bus, ferry and foot. It was an adventure that would introduce me to some of the most eccentric and most incredible people I've ever met. And, like all good adventures, it was also one that would not exactly go to plan.

But right now, I didn't know any of that. All I knew was that I was sitting on a very slow commuter train, trundling along the side of a canal in Lincolnshire.

As settings go, I'll admit this isn't the first place you might expect to start an adventure. Lincolnshire lacks something of the cinematic grandeur you might anticipate for a saga such as…I don't know – *Lord of the Rings*. Or *Thelma and Louise*. But, in my head at least, it didn't make the slightest bit of difference.

As I looked out of the window, I spotted a collection of trailers that had once been used to transport the equipment for an American circus, long since abandoned and left to rust. The thought of jobless clowns would have ordinarily left me feeling a bit sad. But things were moving in an exciting new direction.

I had decided I was going to visit twelve places as a Door-to-Door Poet – one every month. I would approach roughly a hundred people in that time and, out of those people, I was hoping to persuade thirty to let me write a poem for them.

I was aiming to speak to three residents in every place I went to. The only question I was going to ask them was: 'What is important to you?' Once I'd had a conversation about it, I'd travel back home to write the poems, before heading back a few weeks later to deliver them.

In preparation for the trip, I'd been gathering some specialist equipment. I'd bought myself a digital camera. I'd got some business cards printed with a little picture of my briefcase on. I thought this might make the whole thing look a bit more official.

I was interested in speaking to as many individuals as possible. Especially people who lived their lives differently to me. And then we'd find out for sure, wouldn't we? If this project went nationwide, we'd find out whether Cathy was right or not. We'd find out if most people in most parts of the country would stop to talk to a stranger if you approached them in the right way.

I wanted to record the conversations I had too. To make a note of the kinds of subjects that were important to people. And when I considered what kinds of places I could visit that would help me achieve this goal, the first word that sprang to mind was Boston.

That's Boston, UK, by the way, not USA. The 'OG' Boston is a small town in the south of Lincolnshire. Not quite as exotic. But I was very interested in it all the same.

Boston has been dubbed 'The UK's Most Divided Town'. At least, that's how it's been described in the news and on social media. It was the town that voted higher than any other to leave the European Union. There'd been countless reports of tensions between the white working class and the Eastern European communities living there.

It's also a town very near to where Rose grew up, which was what brought it to my attention in the first place. In any other circumstances, I could have stayed with her family when I got there. But I'd forgotten they were coming to visit us in Newcastle that weekend, so we crossed each other on the train tracks like ships in the night.

This was the plan: I was going to try and find a mixture of Eastern European and white British residents to write a poem for. I wasn't going to ask any leading questions. The only question I would ask was: *What is important to you?* But I couldn't help but wonder if some of these issues might come out on their own.

As the train passed through a series of tiny market towns, I was starting to realise this wasn't the North I knew any more. We were now entering something that was still described by some people as the North but, as far as I was concerned, it was definitely The Midlands.

I got off the train at 10:22am. I was immediately struck by how flat everything was. Looking down the tracks, I could see for miles in either direction.

I was reminded of a joke that my stepdad is fond of telling: that Lincolnshire is the only county in England where you can watch your dog running away from you for two days in a row. I started to walk towards the town centre.

I don't know what I was expecting from Boston. Stories in the news had painted a pretty bleak picture. Sepia photos of lonely children. Boarded-up windows and a dirty river. As I strolled down the cobbled streets that morning, past arty cafés and Turkish restaurants, nothing could have seemed further from the truth.

Happy families walked by. Business owners waved to each other in the street. In the town square, I encountered what is affectionately referred to as 'The Stump', one of the largest parish churches in the country.

Standing at eighty metres, its tower reached high up into the clouds above. It could have easily been a cathedral as far as I was concerned, its Gothic pinnacles glowing white in the morning sun. Surely, there is not a more ironically named building in the whole country.

If I was having a weekend away, I'd have considered

wandering inside, stopping off for some tea and scones. But I reminded myself that this was no holiday. Instead, I turned on my heels and set off for Taverner Road.

I'd been feeling a bit nervous about how far Boston was from my original experiment. I hadn't done anything like this before. I was also aware that anything I wrote was going to be filtered. That the story was going to be reflected through the lens of, let's face it, a white, male, liberal arts worker. If I wanted to make a good job of this, I knew I needed a bit of help.

I got to Fenside Community Centre that afternoon, a '70s oblong building with a corrugated steel roof. It was on the outskirts of town, in what I was told was one of Boston's most deprived neighbourhoods.

Inside, I was greeted by Julie, who had offered to introduce me to her friend Wislawa. She gave me a little tour of the place, before leading me through to a computer suite.

A few minutes later, a woman sauntered in wearing a black poncho, black jeans and huge black cowboy boots. The only thing missing was a soundtrack from Ennio Morricone. I felt like I was about to get embroiled in a rooting-tooting show-down.

Wislawa, it turned out, was the most appropriately qualified person I could have hoped to speak to about my concerns that day. I don't think I could have found a more knowledgeable or helpful citizen in the whole town. She told me her job was to help Eastern Europeans who've recently arrived in the country. She explained that she often did door-to-door visits. As a Polish migrant, she knew how difficult it could be arriving in a strange place and not really knowing your way around.

We got ourselves a cup of tea and I went over the plan. I asked Wislawa if there was a good street to try in Boston.

'This one outside,' she said, pointing out of the window. 'There's a big mix of people.'

After this, she went a bit quiet.

'Can I be honest with you?' she said, as we sat facing each other. She looked away for a minute, in the way that people often do when they're breaking some news they know you won't really appreciate.

'I don't think this is going to work here,' she told me. 'With anyone. I'm also quite concerned about your safety.'

But I told Wislawa not to worry. I was, after all, an official Door-to-Door Poet. I knew exactly what I was doing.

Instead, I asked her if there was anything I should avoid saying or doing.

'Not really,' she told me. 'I think the biggest problem you will have is that many people won't speak English.'

We talked about some of the reasons for this. The lack of events, the pressures of work and family, how finding the time and money to learn English can be difficult.

'There are not a lot of opportunities,' Wislawa explained. 'I was studying English in this community centre. When I finished, I felt like I still didn't know very much. I asked my tutor how I could learn more and he told me that you can't. If you have a hunger for knowledge here, you will go hungry.'

Having talked for nearly an hour, I felt a lot more

prepared for some of the challenges I might be up against. I thanked Wislawa for her time, before making my goodbyes and heading off.

That evening, I went for an Indian curry in the town centre, not far from The Stump. In what was quickly turning into something of a pre Door-to-Door-Poetry ritual, I opted for the vegetable dhansak.

In fact, in the following year, I was to go on to sample a vegetable dhansak in a wide array of towns and cities across the country. I learned a lot about the subject. I'd even go as far to say that this is now one of my greatest areas of expertise. Good spice level, lots of pineapple, not too shy on the lentils. If you happen to like a vegetable dhansak, they do a good one in Boston.

Back at the hotel, my thoughts turned to tomorrow and the impending challenge. I ran over the lines of my introductory poem. I made sure my phone was on charge.

Wislawa had refused to let me attempt this without us exchanging numbers first. She had made me promise to give her an update about my progress once an hour, every hour, from the moment I started knocking until I was done.

'I won't be able to live with myself otherwise,' she'd said.

Somewhat inevitably, I'd begun to consider the reasons why.

I was beginning to realise that this was the real test. This would be the first place I'd gone knocking outside of my home town. If it didn't work here, it did not bode well for the rest of the trip.

What if Cathy was right? What if I'd just stepped clean

out of my comfort zone and was about to discover how impossible this really was?

I put on some pyjamas and got into bed. I turned off the light. I lay in the dark for what felt like a very long time.

The Boston Stump

It dominates the sky
like a medieval tower of Babel;
the fortress of Rapunzel,
only built to be less fatal.
And you'll wonder at the craftsmanship,
and then your head will slump
when you find out that someone has named
this church the Boston Stump.

Like the Taj Mahal is a paving stone,
like the Amazon is overgrown,
like the Big Bang was a minor bump,
the naming of the Boston Stump.

Surely no worse moniker
for any place was planned,
since the Canadian town of Swastika
or the frozen plains of Greenland.
When the honour, skill and deep obsession
of those who reached up to the heavens
was flattened like a chopped-down trunk,
the naming of the Boston Stump.

Was it just their sense of humour
or some bitter cynicism?
Was it actually a plot

to stop Americans from visiting?
Some scheme to dodge the planning fees
now past the point of irony?
Shane MacGowan once got drunk,
the naming of the Boston Stump.

4

BOSTON KNOCKING

I WOKE UP ON THE WOBBLY steel frame of the hotel bed. As I opened my eyes, the gravity of the situation pushed down on me, fixed me in place, pressing on my chest like a sack of lead bricks.

For half an hour I lay there, pinned to the mattress, staring at the fool's gold chandelier, wondering exactly what I'd got myself into.

I had opted to spend the night in the New England Hotel. It was central and within my meagre means. But as I struggled to break into motion that morning, the name put me in mind of the song 'A New England' by Billy Bragg. I thought about how, like Billy, I also wasn't looking for a new England – just somewhere warm and clean, with a fried breakfast included in the fee.

The hotel itself had a fading decadence. It was all yellow paisley carpets and Roman-style columns. There was a desk at the entrance with a big brass bell, like something from *Fawlty Towers*. When I'd rung it the day before, a very friendly member of staff had come to check me in.

'Business or pleasure?' she'd asked.

'I'm not really sure,' I replied. 'I'm a Door-to-Door Poet.'

She smiled and carried on, as if I was the third Door-to-Door Poet to have checked in that day.

It was the 6th of April 2019. In the week leading up to this, Theresa May had submitted four proposed options for a Brexit deal to the House of Commons. All of these had been rejected. She'd then written to the EU requesting an extension on the deadline set for us to leave. This had also been rejected. Not good news for the Eurosceptics, I imagined. Or maybe it was. I wasn't really sure. No matter which side of the fence you sat on, I was left feeling like I was at the centre of something.

I forced myself from under the duvet and managed to get dressed. Downstairs, in an otherwise deserted dining area, I ordered my promised fry-up.

'What brings you to Lincolnshire?' the waitress asked. I explained. The conversation went eerily quiet.

I went back upstairs and got ready to leave. I paced around the room, considering some of the day's possible and potentially horrific outcomes. Then I put on my coat, grabbed my briefcase and set off.

It was a chilly, grey afternoon as I left the hotel. The sky was overcast, but there was a jolly atmosphere in the town. It was the first day of the Easter holidays. The cobbled roads were full of families shopping and teenagers vaping without pause.

I strolled across a wrought-iron bridge. I began to walk down a long residential road. A man came speeding past on a mobility scooter, covered head-to-toe in Union Jack bunting. I spotted a bus which had no number and no definite destination. The front simply read 'UP TOWN' and the novelty of this still brings a smile to my face.

I took a right off Laughton Road and arrived at Taverner. Taverner Road was a street of red brick, 1950s, semi-detached houses. They stretched off in front me, before forking in two a little further along. There was a children's play area with some swings in it. Behind me was a service for people in recovery from drug and alcohol problems.

I decided I was going to go all the way up the left-hand side of the street. There were more than enough doors to try. However, as I hovered on the verge of starting, the nerves had just about got the better of me. I could feel the blood rushing around in my ears, my heartbeat drumming in my head. But it was no use standing here, I thought. The time had come to get on with it.

I walked up to the first house and opened the gate. I headed carefully up the garden path, then pressed the bell.

I waited.

The door had a glass pane in it, with an orange curtain hanging over the back. After a moment, the curtain started to twitch. It was a faint twitching. But a definite human movement nonetheless. I felt my pulse speed up a notch.

There was what seemed like a lot of cardboard boxes stacked on the other side of the door. Someone began to move them, slowly, one after the other, the mounting tension reaching nigh on unbearable levels.

After what felt like many minutes, the door sprang open. A lady with red spiky hair and tattoos appeared. I asked if she had a minute. She said yes. I launched into my introductory poem.

'I'm a Door-to-Door Poet, and I know that sounds quite crazy, but—'

'Whoa, whoa, whoa. Just slow down,' she said. 'I'm sorry, but I don't really understand why you're doing this.'

I was hoping the poem might be enough to explain, so I carried on from where I'd left off.

'I'm here to make poetry exciting, like bungee jumping, but less frightening, and—'

'No, sorry. Just stop there a minute. You've just said you don't want any money or anything. And it's not all about the money, obviously. But I don't really understand what you're getting out of this.'

Clearly, the poem was not helping. I decided to change tack.

'Well, I'm trying to show that anyone can enjoy poetry,' I reasoned. 'And that strangers aren't as scary as they're made out to be and—'

'Yeah, OK. But *why* are you doing it?'

'To write poems for people.'

'But why?'

I had completely run out of ways to explain myself. I sheepishly apologised for bothering her, then went on my way.

That's OK, I thought. It was important not to let this rattle me.

I walked out of the gate and along the road to the next house. I headed up the path and rang the bell. An older woman in a wheelchair came out. I told her what it was about.

'NO!' she yelled, before slamming the door. I carried on.

There were a few no answers. A few more nos. On the way, I passed a man painting his fence. He told me he was busy in a tone that suggested I should not hang about.

A few doors down from this, a friendly big-set gentleman in a grey hoodie answered. He had a lovely smile, but told me he couldn't speak any English.

'Poetry?' I said, hoping this might resonate. He shook his head politely. 'Shakespeare?' I tried, in a last-ditch attempt. He shrugged and smiled. He seemed keen to help, but there wasn't much else we could do in the circumstances. I thanked him and carried on up the road.

It had been nearly an hour. I was beginning to get a little worried. It hadn't taken this long to find someone the last time. Everyone I'd spoken to had said they were busy. Or that they didn't speak English. Or that they just didn't understand what I was doing.

What if Wislawa was right? What if it really wasn't going to work here? And if it wasn't going to work here, what did this mean for the rest of the trip?

A wave of panic began to rise slowly, starting in the pit of my stomach, creeping up into my chest. More doors, more disappointments. A man with short brown hair with a cigarette dangling out of his mouth said no very quickly. A lady in a pink and yellow dressing gown told me she couldn't speak English. A woman who looked to be a nonagenarian answered and told me she was too frail to be standing at the door in this weather.

To be fair, this last reply seemed like a very sensible excuse. I was secretly happy to know this woman would be nice and warm inside, instead of risking her life with some obscure poet. But it didn't do much to remedy the situation.

It had now been over an hour. I was beginning to consider how long it would be before I gave up. Exactly how far along this street would I need to get before I decided I'd gone far enough? Where exactly would the mission have failed?

Then I got to a house with a pink blossom tree in the garden. A woman came out. I asked her if she had a minute. She said yes.

I started my introductory poem and she stopped me halfway through.

'I've got something I'd like you to write me a poem about,' she said.

'OK, great,' I replied. 'What is it?'

I'd assumed it would be something breezy and lighthearted, something to match this positive turn of fate. Then the woman said something that changed everything. And as the words dropped out of her mouth, it felt like someone had slammed the brakes on at a hundred miles an hour, my head flying forwards with the colossal force of it.

'My daughter,' she told me. 'She was murdered.'

Mother's Call

She's standing in the garden, by a lilac-blossom tree,
when she tells me it gets harder every day.
Her light blue eyes are empty and wider than the sea,
her voice is calling from a world away.

She starts to tell the story of the stopping of the clocks,
of ground that disappeared beneath her feet,
the day her teenage daughter went out to the corner shops
and was stabbed to death as she walked down the street.

She wants to stand in parliament, address every MP,
just to see if it would even rouse them
as she describes the way they had to drag her from the scene
and how she's only one of many thousands.

To ask them how they'd feel if it was their kid.
Would the police's budget still get chopped?
Would they still squeeze the dregs from all our public services
to fill their crystal glasses to the top?

And she tells me that the nightmare's never over,
to her the moment's playing on repeat,
since the ticking of the second pointer froze,
and the ground, it vanished underneath her feet.

That in her mind, she's standing underneath the blossom tree,
waving to her only little girl,
with cobalt eyes as deep and wide and empty as the sea,
and a voice that's calling from another world.

5

STOCKTON

I STOOD ON MARGARET's doorstep, fumbling for words.

What are you supposed to say?

I kept trying, but nothing would come. I managed a syllable, then a pause. I took a second to compose myself. I tried again. But it was no use.

No matter how many times I tried, there was no reply I could give that would ever sound anything more than irrelevant.

My head was racing in a hundred different directions. I wanted to ask if Margaret was OK. I wanted to say this was unimaginable, horrific and heartbreaking. I wanted to know more about what had happened. But I also didn't want to ask anything that might upset her.

I hadn't even got to the part where I explained that I wanted to record the conversation, that I wanted to write about it. The idea of this poor woman telling me anything more without knowing the full extent of what I was planning to do with it was deeply worrying. I needed to ask her permission.

More than anything else, I just felt really really sorry for her. This was by far the most personal and serious suggestion I could imagine. I had no idea what to say. I still don't.

I managed to clumsily mumble something to this effect. Margaret smiled and told me that it was OK, that it had happened a few years ago, that she felt able to talk about it.

In fact, she told me that she wanted me to record what had happened, every single word of it, so she could spread the message as far as humanly possible.

I learned that Margaret's daughter was called Angela. She was fifteen when she died. The boy who killed her was one year older. He was a friend from school. Margaret believed he must have been planning it for a long time, although the police never found a motive. The boy went to a Young Offenders Institute for five and a half years. Since his release, Margaret had seen him walking in the town where it happened, something that she clearly found very difficult to cope with.

The most upsetting part of all of this from my point of view was that it was still clearly so raw, after all those years. There was no doubt in my mind that this had been the all-consuming force that had governed everything Margaret had done or said since it happened. And who could possibly blame her for that? It was so horrible. I told her I couldn't begin to understand what she'd been through. I thanked her for taking the time to talk. For being so honest.

I went back to Newcastle the next morning. In every place I visited, the plan was to work on the poems at my house, then return to deliver them two weeks later. That evening, in the quiet of my flat, I had plenty of time to think about how stupid I'd really been.

I'd gone to Boston trying to find out about a divided nation. But I wasn't a journalist, was I? I wasn't going around vox popping people in the street about Brexit. How could I possibly have assumed that the only thing anyone would want to talk about would be everything I'd read about in the papers? People aren't caricatures, are they?

The whole interaction reminded me of something I'd already learned. Something I wish I had remembered.

You see, before I set off on this adventure, I'd tested out Door-to-Door Poetry in a few places near where I live, just to make sure that meeting Kyle wasn't a fluke. One of those places had been Stockton-on-Tees.

I think it would be fair to say that Stockon has a bit of a bad reputation. It was once the location for a reality TV show called *Benefits Street,* which was criticised at the time for taking advantage of the local residents.

I'd ended up on a street called Hartington Road, which was described to me, on three separate occasions, as 'the roughest street in Stockon'.

It was a row of massive three-storey Victorian terraces, with huge bay windows and elaborately crested finials. In fact, I found out later that it used to be a very well-to-do area, lived in by doctors and lawyers before the decline of the local trades. Since then, the houses had been split up into flats, with some now used as a service for people who were homeless. A lot of the doors were boarded up, the paintwork in a thorough state of flaking.

I was a bit scared. But, on a deeper level, I felt like I knew

57

how this was going to pan out. I was going to find someone who fitted the profile of a stereotypical Stockton resident. I was going to hear their opinions on how the town had been portrayed. We'd get a bit of insight into the reasons someone might need benefits, and I'd be able to show another side of the story.

What happened in the end was very different indeed.

As I stood outside the first house, preparing to ring one of an infinitesimal number of doorbells, a man approached me with thick-rimmed glasses and neat grey hair combed to the side. He looked a bit like the philosopher and linguist Noam Chomsky.

'Are you looking for someone?' he asked.

I explained.

'Poetry?' he said. 'I love poetry. You'd better come in.'

It wasn't exactly the response I'd been expecting.

I followed the man through the hallway, up a staircase with a big oak banister, and into his flat. He showed me into his living room, which was covered with mahogany shelves filled with Dickens and Chaucer. I sat down in his plush leather armchair, in front of the writing desk, complete with pots of ink and vellum paper. He brought us both a cup of freshly brewed coffee.

This was Boris and he was a total intellectual. We raced through all kinds of subjects that day. We put the world to rights. Boris told me that he liked to record birdsong. I told him I think birdsong is kind of fascinating.

'Scientifically, it's for mating and establishing territory,' he said. 'But if you're into more spiritual things…'

Boris explained that he was raised a Roman Catholic.

'Indoctrinated, really.'

But he'd gone on to study a whole load of other religions: Hinduism, Islam, Buddhism.

'The main thing I've learned is to treat other people the way you'd like to be treated. It doesn't always work, mind. But it's worth trying.'

We talked for an hour about everything under the sun. The poetry of Kipling. Whether cruelty is inherently ingrained into us as a species. Is there intelligent life out there? If so, what would they make of us?

After my second cup of coffee, I thanked Boris for his time. It had reminded me how important it was to keep an open mind.

As I got ready to leave, I noticed a briefcase on the floor next to the fireplace. I told Boris I liked it. It was a bit like mine, only much fancier. It was shinier for a start, and it folded open at the top like an old-fashioned doctor's bag. I felt like I'd been searching for a briefcase like this my whole life. Of course, I didn't say that to Boris at the time.

'Oh, I just use it to put paperwork in,' he told me. 'You should have it.'

I felt embarrassed. My eyes must have greedily given away my thoughts. I told Boris that this was very kind of him, but I couldn't possibly take his briefcase.

'No, go on,' he insisted. 'Why don't you put your things in and see how it feels?'

After a bit of polite toing and froing, we agreed to do a swap. Boris even got hold of some fishing line and fixed the hole in my original briefcase, before trying to give it back to me. But it felt right that he should keep it for himself. He'd already given more than enough to me.

It was a heartwarming encounter. But it didn't all go the way I was hoping. Between meeting Boris and heading back to deliver his poem, I was contacted by a news crew who wanted to film my poetry deliveries. I had rung Boris to see if this might be something he was interested in. It turns out it wasn't. And, what's more, the idea of it had made him quite anxious.

He told me that the town had already suffered enough misrepresentation. He told me that he thought it would be best if I deleted everything I'd recorded. That he didn't want to be a part of this any more.

I tried to explain that this wasn't the reason I'd come. That I could return with the poem on my own, as planned. But the damage had already been done. And things were now moving in a direction I could no longer control.

'I should probably tell you something, Rowan,' he said. 'I suffer from some quite serious mental health issues. When people find out the name of my condition, they get scared. I don't really go out very much, I don't see anyone.'

In the end, we managed to smooth things over. Boris got in touch a few weeks later to ask if I could deliver his poem on my own. When I went back, we swapped some books and agreed to go out for some tea and cake in the not-too-distant future. It was a happier ending than it might have been.

But the whole interaction was a sobering lesson. It taught me that you can't make any assumptions as a Door-to-Door

Poet. When you're approaching a stranger's door, you need to be prepared for the whole spectrum of what you might find on the other side.

After that meeting with Boris, I'd made a promise to myself: from this point forward, I'd keep an open mind at all times. I'd never go looking for anyone in particular. I'd let the people on the doorsteps speak for themselves.

Clearly, I had completely forgotten that promise.

I was due to go back to Boston to deliver Margaret's poem on the 20th of April. In the wee hours of the morning, I reached over to check the time on my phone. It was 4am. As I stared up at the ceiling, I thought again about what I'd written, and about the way Margaret might feel about it.

How could I ever do this subject any justice? I felt like I was in way over my head.

Still, whatever the outcome, writing Margarets' poem had brought me up to person number four on my mission to find thirty citizens. There were some other people in Boston as well. As I'm sure you can appreciate, I spoke to more individuals on this journey than there is going to be space to talk about here. Suffice to say, other residents of Taverner Road included Pauline, who was a big fan of banger racing, an extreme sport that involves crashing souped-up cars into each other at great speed, and Tracey, who, like Boris, was very open about her mental health issues.

And even if I wasn't really sure what I was doing here, Margaret had been so honest with me. She had put her faith in a total stranger and had dared to share one of the most private and painful experiences of her life with me. If Margaret could find the courage to do this, despite everything that had happened to her, I knew I owed it to her and the other people I'd met so far to find a way to keep going as well.

As the sun began to rise, I got out of bed, having lain awake the entire night. I got dressed, picked up my briefcase and set off for the train station. I didn't know where this journey was leading me any more. All I knew was that I needed to keep moving.

All Ears

I understand it can be hard to find the moment
when the people asking how you are
don't really want to know.
When the truth evokes a sharp and awkward silence,
sometimes, you say, it's easier to hide it.

In this world where every rosy-cheeked achievement
is dusted off with glitter and pasted on each wall.
In this world where every illness is a weakness,
a face that's only shown behind a door.

And you tell me you don't want to be a burden,
when everybody's futures are ballooning by the day,
you don't want to be the one to stick the pin in.
And I'm trying to find the language to explain

I don't want you to bend your life around mine.
I'm here because I love you as a whole,
through every apocalyptic thunderstorm,
through every day that seems to be on mute.

I've always got a pair of ears for you,
no matter what you're holding underneath.
Believe me when I say that anytime is fine,
and when I ask you how you are
I really mean it.

6

MANCHESTER

I DIDN'T KNOW MUCH ABOUT England when I started this journey. But my next stop was an exception to that rule. I've got a few friends in Manchester. I'd visited various times over the years to see them and to sample the city's copious nightlife.

In some ways, this made the trip there feel more reassuring, though I wasn't sure if it would make much difference when it came to knocking on doors.

I woke up on the 17th of May and boarded the first train from Newcastle. It wasn't exactly through choice.

I have never been a morning person. It's a productive day for me if I manage to crawl out of bed by 9am. Even then, I need a pint of tea and a good long stare at the wall before I'm able to so much as string a sentence together.

Somewhat predictably then, I'd slept in, and the resulting dash to the station had got me there with barely a minute to spare before the doors folded shut and the train pulled away.

I found my seat. After finally catching my breath, I took a minute to look out at the world speeding past beyond the window. To consider my chosen mode of transport.

I was planning on doing most of this trip by rail. On the one hand, I didn't really have much choice. I can't drive, and the hiring of a personal chauffeur, though it would have been very welcome, is beyond the limits of the average bard's salary.

But I'd told myself this would be kind of symbolic, too. Surely it was the perfect form of travel for a Door-to-Door Poet. 'The transport of the people'. Not only would I be learning about a wide variety of citizens on their doorsteps, I'd be doing it on the Great British Railway as well. You would assume the conversations I had with people on the trains themselves would be just as interesting as the ones I had on the doorsteps. Maybe even more so.

In reality, the five journeys I'd taken so far had been a stark reminder that people really hate talking on public transport. Really, though. The average English person will walk through molten lava if it means avoiding eye contact with a fellow passenger. And I am no exception to this rule, either. Especially when I've jumped on a carriage at 6.42 in the morning.

The seats that day were scattered with commuters, cowering in corners, wrapped in headphones, trying to soothe the pain of the now frighteningly bright sunrise bursting through the grassy fields beyond. And fair play to them, I thought. Maybe we don't need to be talking all of the time. It's nice to have a moment of peace every now and again, isn't it?

I knew we were approaching Manchester when I spotted the huge glass tower blocks on the horizon. I got off at

Victoria station and wove through a crowd of people.

As with Boston, I'd arrived early for my mission. I was planning to spend the afternoon with my friend Bee, before going knocking the following day.

I was going to try Door-to-Door Poetry in a place called Moss Side.

The words 'Moss' and 'Side' have become synonymous with gangs and violence over the years. A talk with some Manchester residents in the weeks leading up to my visit had led me to wonder if this estate was really as dangerous as it might once have been. But there was no denying that, when I quizzed a handful of locals about what I was planning, their responses were pretty mixed. They ranged from comments such as *brilliant, you'll have a lovely time,* to *this is the roughest area in Manchester and I really don't think you should do this.*

As I passed through the city that day, it did feel like the stakes had been raised here. Whatever your feelings about Moss Side, I was now entering a metropolis for the first time as a Door-to-Door Poet. The population was much greater, the people, I assumed, much busier. I was starting to worry about the way this could affect my chances.

I arrived at Bee's house later that morning. She was living in a basement flat at the time and had recently got a new puppy. She was a black labrador called Frida, and I spent the rest of the day watching her wriggle around the house like a gangly eel. That evening, we went out for some Thai food with a group of friends. I had suggested an Indian, to allow for the customary dhansak, but I was outvoted.

In the morning, I woke up in Bee's spare room. I got ready to leave and she drove me over to Moss Side. I was now feeling pretty skittish, so I was grateful to have someone there for moral support. Also, Bee is a big fan of house music, and the repetitive booming of the stereo as it blasted Andrew Weatherall records at top volume did something to distract me from my worries, at least for the duration of the journey.

We passed along the ironically named Moss Lane, a very busy A road that resembles a lane in the same way a jumbo jet resembles a paper aeroplane. We took a left into Moss Side, onto a street called Quinney Crescent. I got out of the car and waved goodbye to Bee.

'I'm going to be finished by 6pm,' I told her. 'If you don't hear from me by then, send help.'

She drove off, leaving me standing there, feeling as small and silly as the first day of school.

By this point, Manchester felt so exceptionally massive that the idea of doing Door-to-Door Poetry here was frankly laughable. Surely no one in Moss Side was going to take this seriously. What did I think I was trying to do here?

The estate was encircled by a row of terraced houses. They were made of yellow brick. The row was long and tall and distinctly quadrilateral, like a castle wall. Even the windows seemed to be joining in with this pantomime. They were thin as arrow slits – so much so that I wondered how they could possibly be letting any light in. I felt like I'd landed outside the fortress of some dystopian militia.

I took a minute to get my bearings. On my right were

the houses. On my left was a patch of grass and some cherry trees. Beyond that was the busy road of Moss Lane, the sound of traffic and police sirens.

I decided I was going to work my way along this outer wall, heading due south. I was hoping to find three people but, at this stage, I would have been more than happy with just one. As I stood there taking in my surroundings, a car with tinted windows drove past very slowly. I had the distinct feeling that the driver was checking me over, trying to decide what I was about.

What did they think I was up to? And what might they do to me if they weren't happy about it? In the circumstances, it didn't really bear thinking about.

I opened the gate of the first house and walked up to a blue door, the wall-like structure now towering above me. I noticed that every doorstep was covered with a little white awning to keep off the rain. This looked so small in comparison to the sheer obelisk of the building that it could easily have been a birdhouse.

I knocked on the letterbox and started to count to forty-five in my head.

I heard a voice coming from an upstairs window.

'Yes?'

I took a few steps back and peered up to the top of the wall. I could just about make out a face.

'Hi, my name's Rowan and I'm doing an art project. Have you got a minute?'

'Yeah, OK,' said the voice, without moving.

'Do you want to maybe come down?'

A middle-aged man appeared at the door with short cropped hair, a white t-shirt and blue shorts. I never found out his name, but he asked to be referred to as 'The Specialist'.

I showed The Specialist my introductory poem. He smiled.

'You've come to the right house,' he said, shaking my hand. 'This is freestyle. Do you know what freestyle means?'

I told him I wasn't sure.

'The way you're approaching people in the street like this. It's like stopping your gran in the road and asking her if she could do a dance. And then she says, "OK, but only if you have 'Blue Suede Shoes' by Elvis Presley." So you start looking through your phone and then...'

At this, The Specialist proceeded to do his best Elvis dance, wiggling his hips and shaking his arms on the doorstep.

My first impressions were that The Specialist was a bit of an eccentric. Then again, considering what had led me here in the first place, I wasn't really one to judge.

I asked The Specialist what was important to him.

'I'd have to say injustice,' he replied.

We began to talk about loneliness, about the way technology can make this worse.

'These days, people can be lonely in a house full of people,' he noted. And then he started to talk about estates.

In The Specialist's opinion, neighbourhoods like Moss Side were bad for people's wellbeing.

'It's a project. And you'll always get that in places like this. The whole layout of the housing here stops people from socialising. Look around you. Where are people supposed to gather?'

'When they designed this place,' he said, 'humanity never really came into it. The most human it got was when the architect went home and had a burger with his wife.'

It was a very moving speech. As a suggestion for a poem, it felt like a gift.

And then The Specialist paused for a moment. He looked away, then turned back to me with an expression of total warmth and earnestness. 'I'll tell you what,' he said, pointing his finger in the air. 'And you can put this on the record...'

If I was sitting on a seat, I would now have been on the edge of it.

What wisdom was The Specialist about to impart? What nugget of truth and insight could he add to what had already been such a powerful suggestion?

'When you first knocked on this door,' he told me, 'I thought you were an 18th-century time traveller. Like something from the *Twilight Zone*.'

Tea with the Time Traveller

I was in the house the other day,
just hoovering the floor,
when this 18th-century time traveller
came knocking at the door.

White curly hair, a cocked hat,
a tailcoat long and purple,
a frilly shirt and stockings
like The Scarlet Pimpernel.

He said his time machine had broke,
he needed some assistance,
could he come in and see the toolbox
and would I help him fix it?

I said I'm sorry to let you down,
but we've never met before
and I've just spilt a load of Quavers
on the living room floor.

He said: *Please sir, I'm begging you,*
I've made a huge mistake,
I came here to view the wonders
of the future human race,

I thought I'd find utopia,
all creatures would be free,
but this world seems more unequal
than 1783.

The rich are so much greedier,
the hungry so much more so,
the towers are so dirty
and no one says hello.

When I ran back to my time machine
to try and ride it home
some youths were leaping round it
and pelting it with stones.

I said it's nowt to do with me mate,
no one can help you here,
I've got a load of crisps to pick up
and I'm not an engineer.

Well, he seemed to get the message,
but as he turned around
I glimpsed his desperate face,
the way his head went drooping down.

I said hang on, wait, I'm sorry,
maybe I've been a little cruel.
Why don't you come in
and I'll see what I can do?

So I led him down the hallway
into the living space,
and he gazed around in wonder
at the gadgets of our age.

He picked up the remote
and I was going to make some tea,
when he pulled off his wig and cried
We knew it! We knew you had a telly!

We've got you now Mr McCabe,
no one escapes our plans!
And that's how I got busted
by the TV licence man.

7

GRANTCHESTER

After talking to The Specialist, I met a man called Nigel. He asked for a poem about nutritional foods. Shortly after this, I spoke to a woman called Mikela, who asked for one about Ancient Egypt.

It didn't take long to find them. And I suppose, with the benefit of hindsight, it makes sense that, if this worked in a place like Boston or Stockton, it would work somewhere like Manchester too.

My experience in Moss Side had been a welcome source of encouragement. And it had persuaded me to try something that felt a lot riskier. Something very different to what I'd been doing so far.

It was now the 13th of June 2019. Theresa May had just resigned as the prime minister. Boris Johson had launched his leadership campaign. And I was a few miles south of Cambridge, very south of Newcastle.

Grantchester is definitely 'The South'. There is no doubt about that. There wasn't a single Greggs in a twenty-mile radius. I had left my big coat and jumper at home. And I couldn't shake the feeling that I was doing something illegal.

That, at any moment, the police would arrive and I'd be bundled into the back of a van and beaten within an inch of my life. I hadn't even knocked on a single door.

Since visiting Moss Side, I'd started to notice a bit of a pattern in the kinds of places I'd been travelling to. I was wondering if it might have something to do with where I come from.

I grew up in a place called Hebburn in South Tyneside. It's only five miles away from where I live now, but it feels a lot further some days.

My current home is the kind of area that's described by estate agents as 'up-and-coming'. You know the sort of place I mean. There's cafés with more than one kind of tea. There's a cinema built and run by anarchists.

By contrast, Hebburn has valiantly resisted all attempts to be gentrified. Landmarks from my youth included a fountain that was never turned on, a pet shop with no pets in it and a takeaway famous for its miscellaneous 'meat special'.

I spent my childhood on an estate on the outskirts of town. I lived with my mam, Lisa, who is a primary-school teacher, and my stepdad, Stephen, who's a cleaner.

Walsh Avenue wasn't exactly a fun place to grow up. But it was home. And it's meant that similar kinds of places have always felt like home too. Even if I've never been there before.

I was beginning to wonder if this was influencing my choice of locations as a Door-to-Door Poet. And I decided I was going to do something to change that.

Grantchester, unlike Hebburn, is a quintessential English

village. It is a Beatrix Potter story, with humans instead of mice. There's country manors with thatched roofs, gardens stuffed with foxgloves. Lamp posts that look like something from the land of Narnia.

If the South was meant to be a hard sell for Door-to-Door Poetry, this was the thick end of the wedge, to say the least. On the train journey down, I'd noticed something was a little awry when I tuned into some of the conversations that were happening around me. A couple of young women were discussing how many abbeys they had visited. A group of students were talking about the relationship between beauty and mathematics. I was a long way from home, Toto.

I took the last leg of the journey by taxi. The driver asked what the address was and I told him I didn't have one yet. He sounded confused.

'What do you mean you don't have an address?'

'It's a bit of a long story,' I said.

I got out of the car in the centre of the village, next to a pub called The Green Man. The sun was beating down and, as I surveyed the picturesque scene around me, I couldn't imagine a day where the sun had not shone on a place like this.

There was just one country lane that wove its way through the village. There were dwellings scattered along the road: cottages and country houses. A little further along, I could make out a church that was once written about by the war poet Rupert Brooke.

In his poem 'The Old Vicarage, Grantchester', there's some famous lines about the clock at the top of this church.

It is described as standing at 'ten to three'. Imagine my disappointment then as I got closer, only to learn that it actually stood at 12.04.

Grantchester is a pretty literary place. Sylvia Plath and Ted Hughes wrote about the meadows nearby, Lord Byron used to go swimming in the river. The list of visitors to the local tea rooms reads like a who's who from a GCSE anthology: Virginia Woolfe, JB Priestley, John Betjeman, etc.

For the first time in my life, I felt underqualified to be a Door-to-Door Poet. I'm not sure if you can be underqualified for a job you've invented for yourself, but that is the way Grantchester had left me feeling. It was the most affluent and intimidating place I had ever visited.

I began to follow the path as it wound its way through the village, heading past the church, beside a hedge that partially obscured a large country garden. Through the leaves of this hedge, I spotted a statue in the shape of a bald faun. It had an almost farcically large penis. I had no idea what, if anything, this was supposed to represent.

In a few minutes, I reached a huge, red-brick Victorian building that was covered in ivy. My research told me that this building had once belonged to Rupert Brooke. But it now belonged to Jeffrey Archer. As I got closer to the building, I saw something that made me stop in my tracks. I came to an actual halt, shocked, confused, trying to process exactly what was happening.

Because something very frightening and unexpected had just come into view: the gates were open. They were actually open. And I was now faced with the possibility of writing a poem for Jeffrey Archer.

In case anyone's wondering, Jeffrey Archer is a novelist and a disgraced Tory politician who may (or may not) have embezzled thousands of pounds of charity money. Grantchester had first come to my attention largely through a funny anecdote that involved the Archers and this very house.

One day I'd met up with my friend James. While we talked of this and that, he'd regaled me with the story of a New Year's Eve party he'd been to in Grantchester, in a house that once belonged to the band Pink Floyd. Knowing chez Archer was close, the night had culminated in James joining an inebriated high-stakes mission to sneak into the Archers' garden and steal some of their coveted figs.

Of course, my plan wasn't *all* about Jeffrey Archer. Like most things in life, the decision had largely come about without any consideration of Jeffrey Archer whatsoever. But I was looking to really step out of my comfort zone, to take the project in a different direction. And the more I spoke to James that day, the more it felt like Grantchester was the perfect place to try this.

That was, at least, until I found myself actually standing outside Jeffrey Archer's house that fine June afternoon.

You see, deep down, I didn't really think this was going to work here. Not with Jeffrey Archer, and not with anyone else in Grantchester either. I wasn't a hundred per cent sure what had made it work so far, but I reasoned it was probably something to do with the kinds of places I'd been visiting. The whole experience was starting to feel like one big, strange fluke. And I had now found myself wanting to know exactly how far I could push my luck before it completely ran out for good.

So what better place to do this than Grantchester? A location that is not only in The South, where I'd already been assured this would not work, but a place that, even compared to other areas in The South, felt particularly challenging.

I mean this with no disrespect to the people of Grantchester, but I felt certain that no one would want speak to me here. We were just too different. We would have nothing in common. And, even if we did have something in common, the odds that we'd actually come into contact with one another seemed slim-to-none. There would be, I imagined, a lot of expensive equipment in place, designed with the sole purpose of keeping out anyone who wasn't a trusted guest. There would be tall fences, barbed wire, security.

This was the real reason I'd come to Grantchester. To fail. And, by failing, to get some kind of a handle on what the limitations of Door-to-Door Poetry actually looked like.

But as I stood at the entrance to Jeffrey Archer's house that day, looking at the ivy-covered brickwork and the latticed windows, this whole idea fell down on itself like a poorly stacked tower of cards.

I'd assumed there'd be an intercom. I'd assumed I would ring it and say, *Hi. Is Jeffrey Archer there?* I'd assumed someone would ask me if I had an appointment. And I would say, *No, but I really want to write him a poem.* And then they'd ask me to leave.

But there was no intercom. The gates were completely open. And I had no idea what I was going to do next.

Did I actually want to meet Jeffrey Archer? What would I say to him if I did? What if we made friends and started going out to the Ascot together? Or sailing yachts off the Italian riviera?

These are some of the many questions you might ask yourself before you travel 120 miles to knock on Jeffrey Archer's front door. In reality, the possibility of meeting him had felt so remote that they'd only really started to cross my mind at this imminent stage.

I suppose the idea of being turned down by Jeffrey Archer wasn't the thing that scared me the most. It was that people like me didn't really belong in a place like this. We simply weren't meant to be here. Were we?

Fuck it.

I stepped through Jeffrey Archer's gates and into his drive. To my left was a big white fountain. Behind it, a silver sports car. I crunched carefully along the gravel and headed towards the door.

The door itself was a wide, Gothic affair made entirely of dark oak. It had a knocker in the shape of a child's head. Next to this was a big rope. I tried tapping on the knocker, but it occurred to me that, in a house of this size, it would probably be a bit hard to hear this, so I pulled the rope straight after. A big brass bell started to ring from somewhere deep inside the premises. The sound reverberated through the whole building. It was an ominous, booming noise – one that seemed to shake my whole body and all the stonework around me, like the trumpeting on the last day of reckoning. I could make out the faint sound of dogs barking, then the quick crunching of footsteps on the gravel.

I spun around and was immediately confronted by a middle-aged woman in an orange cardigan. She jumped when she saw me.

'Hello there,' I stammered. 'My name is Rowan and I don't want any money or anything. I'm going all around the country writing poems for people, for free, on any subject they like, and I was wondering if Jeffrey Archer might be available?'

'He's not in town at the minute, sadly,' she said.

'Oh, that's OK. Would you like a poem instead?'

'I'm just the cleaner,' she said, smiling.

'That's fine. I could still write a poem for you if you like?'

'No thanks,' she replied, in a tone which had now changed to polite-but-firm.

I made my goodbyes and left.

Standing on the country lane again, I felt out of place and completely ridiculous. What the hell did I think I was going to accomplish here? Of course she wasn't interested. This wasn't going to work in Grantchester.

Do you know that Grantchester has the highest concentration of Nobel Prize winners in the world? And there's something about knocking on a potential Nobel Prize winner's door that really makes you scrutinise what you're doing.

I'd been thinking about my introductory poem. I'd realised some of the rhymes in there weren't really 'proper' rhymes. In all the time I'd been doing this, it hadn't seemed to matter. But it really did now, so I'd changed it.

I began to walk back towards the centre of the village,

trying to work up the courage to knock at the different buildings I passed along the way. The next house was a mansion that looked like the set from *The Fresh Prince of Bel Air*. As I walked up the garden path, past the tennis courts and towards the front porch, I was half-expecting a young Will Smith himself to answer, trademark luminous shorts and all. But there was no reply and, instead, I trudged back into the lane defeated.

A few minutes later I got to a white brick mansion that stood behind a twenty-foot sycamore tree. I walked up the path and tapped on the knocker. A man with short white hair and a beard came out. I explained the premise, fully expecting him to make his excuses and say goodbye.

To my surprise, he told me he had a minute.

I started my introductory poem. But in all the excitement, I couldn't remember the changes I'd made, so I just used the old version instead. Surely it wouldn't matter. No one had ever complained about the rhymes in it before.

'"Trace" and "grey" don't really rhyme you know,' he joked, once I'd finished.

'I had a better rhyme but I forgot it,' I told him sheepishly, like a child who's lost their homework.

But despite my loose approach to rhyme, he said he was interested. I could hardly contain my delight.

He told me his name was Ian. I asked him what was important to him.

It turned out that Ian was an architect. He was also a rock-climbing instructor. As if to prove it, he proceeded to get out his business card. It had a picture of him scaling a mountain on it, next to the words: *Qualified to Instruct Adults and Children in Rock Climbing, Indoor Climbing and Abseiling.* I passed Ian my card in return, to prove that I'm a Door-to-Door Poet, qualified in musing, versing and clunky rhyming.

Ian told me he'd just started building an eco-home. He invited me around the back of the house to look at it.

It was a barn-shaped structure made of long grey beams. Ian said he'd been building environmentally friendly homes like this since 1978. I asked if there was a specific moment when he became passionate about this kind of thing.

'In the '70s, there was an oil crisis,' he explained. 'I remember thinking that energy is in short supply, that we oughtn't to be using so much of it. This was before the idea that carbon dioxide was destroying the atmosphere.'

Ian started to talk about the environmental benefits of an eco-home. How it would supply energy back into the grid.

What I liked about him was his realism. His practicality. Ian wasn't a man with his head in the clouds. Like the best rock-climbing instructors, his feet were safely on terra firma.

'Of course,' he said, 'building just one of these isn't really going to make a difference. What we need to do is get everyone living in houses like this. And the only way we're going to be able to do that is if we put some serious pressure on the government.'

Curious, I asked Ian what he thought of protest groups like Extinction Rebellion.

'Well, I think it's very important,' he said. 'We can't sit around and wait for the government to address this crisis any longer. The time to act is now.'

Extinction

Five years,
we've got less than five years.
They're opening coal mines,
nobody cares.
While the ice caps dissolve
and we're facing the floods,
they're expanding Heathrow
like they're still unaware.

Or fracking,
or scrapping renewable energies,
ignoring the biblical droughts and tsunamis.
Pushing reusable bottles in shops
like it'll stop the air choking
or bring back the crops.
It's not nearly enough.
We're in the last days.
They set targets, ignore them,
it all stays the same.
There's only one answer,
one way to make change.
I'm going to superglue myself
to the prime minister's face.

For our children,
it's the only move forward,
I'm joining the new wave of civil disorder.
I'm going to dress like a polar bear,
lie down in the roads,
I'm going to run into parliament
and tear off my clothes.

I don't care if
I end up in prison.
I don't care if
it doesn't make a difference.
We're facing the whole human race's extinction,
I'd rather go mental than sign a petition.

I'm starting today,
I've made my decision,
I'm no Che Guevara,
no Gandhi, no Parks.
But this needs to be done,
it's the end of the line.
This world is our home
and we've run out of time.

8
LUNDY: PART ONE

GRANTCHESTER COMPLETELY MOVED the goalposts. After Ian, I spoke to a man called Vladimir, who lived on the opposite side of the village, near a pub called the Blue Ball Inn. He was a lecturer at Cambridge University and was a big fan of Pink Floyd. He asked for a poem about the meadows nearby.

I could probably have found more people in Grantchester, but after I met Vladimir, I decided to take a walk along the river Cam to see if I could find someone who lived on a houseboat.

Suffice to say, I walked for two hours and found absolutely no one, except a man who was sitting under a tree, chopping up some dog food with a bowie knife. I approached the man and he told me, in no uncertain terms, that he did not have any interest in my little poetry project. He also explained exactly what he would do with the knife if I didn't leave, post-haste.

Bowie knives aside, the trip to Grantchester had gone much better than I was expecting. I wasn't any closer to knowing what the limits of Door-to-Door Poetry were. But that didn't seem to matter so much any more. I felt free. Free to travel wherever I wanted.

Back at home, I'd now written poems for ten people. And it was around this point that Door-to-Door Poetry began to completely take over my life.

It came as a bit of a surprise. At least to me, anyway.

I was sitting in Newcastle City Library, where I'd taken to working through the days. I'd probably been in there a bit too much recently. I think you know you've been spending too long in a building when you begin to learn the comings and goings of the cleaning staff, or when they start tidying around you and letting you stay till the lights are turned off.

I love Newcastle Library. It's my favourite place to get stuff done. It's one of those buildings made entirely of glass. It's full of light. On the top floor there's a viewing platform with some pink swivelly chairs with huge backs on them. You can look down at the tiny people on the streets below, at all their miniscule comings and goings. It makes me feel like a cross between Alan Bennett and Lex Luther.

By this point it was the end of July. Rose had just started her summer holidays. Through the daytime, she would go shopping in town and we'd meet up for an hour in the library café and try to spend something that looked like quality time together.

Things had been a bit busy.

The idea was to visit one place at the start of every month, to come home and spend two weeks writing the poems, before heading back to make the deliveries. Those two weeks were supposed to give me more than enough time to finish the poems. They were also supposed to give me a bit of time to get on with the rest of my life. Time to rest, to see family and friends.

In reality, Door-to-Door Poetry had started to dominate my every waking moment. It was all 'Door-to-Door Poetry this', 'Door-to-Door Poetry that'. And the weirdest bit about this was that the whole thing had begun to feel kind of normal. On the rare occasions I did go out, people would ask me what I did with myself and I'd tell them, completely matter-of-fact, like I was informing them I worked in a legal firm, or a paperclip factory.

I'd even started to feel a little irritated when they sounded surprised. I was forgetting there was ever a time when I did anything apart from knocking on stranger's doors. This is not ideal for a person's mental wellbeing.

It was during one of our slightly rushed dates that Rose sat down in the library café and brought up what should have been a fairly straightforward question.

'Listen, Rowan, I've been trying to find the right time to ask you this. This Door-to-Door Poetry thing. Where exactly is this all going?'

I took a big sip of my coffee. I honestly had no idea.

I'd got hold of a grant to do it for a year. I'd managed to persuade the Arts Council to give me some money. But I knew I didn't want to do this forever. What I was looking for was some kind of conclusion. An ending. I didn't know what that might look like yet. All I knew was that I couldn't stop until I'd found it.

But, Rose, quite understandably, wanted to think a little further ahead than that. She wanted to know what my plans were for, you know, the future and stuff. And she was getting a bit concerned about the amount of time I was spending on all of this.

'You're working really long hours,' she pointed out.

I nodded.

'And you're not really getting paid very much for that.'

I nodded again. God bless the Arts Council but, if I told them how long this was actually going to take, I don't think they'd have ever given me the money.

'I almost wouldn't mind if you were available every so often,' she said. 'But I'm sick of telling all our friends that you can't make it to things. I'm tired of meeting up with everyone on my own.'

It was all a very fair point.

One thing I hadn't really accounted for was the planning. As I got further and further away from home, arranging the trips was getting more complicated. It was the figuring out where to go, the asking people who lived there for advice, booking the trains and looking into the bus routes.

There were some other unexpected delays too. Like when I went back to deliver Ian's poem and he wasn't in. I decided to wait an extra day, so I could go back and read it out to him in person.

Rose found this incredibly confusing.

'You're spending an extra day in a town you barely know, on your own, to try and meet a man you've met once before, who wasn't in when you called on him in the first place?'

From the outside, I could understand how mental that sounded.

But I felt very aware that no one had tried anything like this before. That once it was done, it was done. I wanted to make a good job of it. But it was beginning to feel like I'd bitten off a bit more than I could really chew.

I looked up at this beautiful woman, this woman who had tolerated my ridiculous, hair-brained schemes for eight years of her life. Who'd been there to comfort me through the failures, to share in the joys.

In that moment, I wanted to sack the whole thing off. I wanted to take her out to the pictures, or on a spontaneous holiday. But I couldn't. Not right now. There were commitments. There were things I'd said I'd do and there was no way of getting out of them. It felt like I'd been sucked up by this big snowball that kept rolling faster and faster and I couldn't make it slow down, no matter how hard I tried.

I promised Rose that it wouldn't be too long before this was over. I promised that, once it was over, I would sit down and figure out what I was going to do with the rest of my life. I also promised I'd be around a bit more in the meantime, too.

'Do you really promise?' she said. 'Because my parents are visiting in September and it would mean a lot to me if you were here.'

'I promise,' I said. And, with that, she left me sitting in the library, beavering away at my ridiculous scribblings.

July came and went. I kept knocking on doors. I knocked on doors through August, as children spent meandering afternoons in parks across the land. I knocked as the evenings got a little darker, as the first signs of autumn began to creep into the edges of the nights.

And, on the 5th of September, a few days after Rose had gone back to work, a group of Extinction Rebellion activists were busy gluing themselves to the floor of a Barclays Bank, while I had found myself standing at a port in Ilfracombe, about to board a boat to Lundy Island.

I was waiting with a crowd with seventy other passengers. It was windy and cold. It had started to rain. I pulled my coat collar up around my face as the waves crashed into the pier beside me.

The boat, the MS Oldenburg, was a restored 20th-century German steam vessel. Its vintage nature made me feel a bit like I was in *Shutter Island* with Leonardo DiCaprio.

When I'd arrived that morning, I'd gone over to the harbour master's office, a little red-brick cube of a building. I was informed by a member of staff that I'd have to check in my rucksack, which would then be loaded into a wooden crate with the rest of the passengers' bags.

I now watched as a pneumatic crane began to lift one of these crates off the ground, over into the ferry's hull. The box was wobbling in the rough weather as it dangled mid-air between the land and the sea. I was surprised it wasn't blown away.

I wasn't sure I'd even make it this far. I'd been told the crossing in the Bristol Channel could be choppy and unpredictable. There was no way of guaranteeing the boat would even run until the evening before the trip. So the previous night, I'd sat on the edge of my hotel bed and dialled the number of the ferry company. An automated message had played, informing me in a soothing West Country accent that the weather forecast was fair and the journey would proceed as planned.

I love the West Country accent, me. I always have. I can't imagine any news coming across as bad in a voice like that.

Imagine some of the worst news you could ever receive.

'I'm sorry, but we're going to have to put her down.'

Now imagine that news in a West Country accent. Does it still sound like bad news? Of course it doesn't. Not when it's relayed by a cross between a farmer and a pirate.

And remember, I can say that because I have a silly accent. I've taken the liberty of translating this entire story into Standard English, or at least as close to it as I can get. Face-to-face, I was often mistaken for offering 'Door-to-Door Poultry', a project which I'm sure would have been much more enthusiastically received, even if it didn't align with my vegetarian principles.

With everything going to plan, I'd awoken the next morning at the Royal Brittania Hotel. I'd cashed in on my complimentary fry-up, before heading out to start the day's adventure.

Wandering over to the edge of the pier, I'd passed various shops with brightly painted signs proclaiming 'Ice Cream' and 'Fudge 'n' Things'. I passed a sculpture made by Damien Hirst, a thirty-foot statue of a pregnant woman holding a sword and scales.

She was standing on top of a pile of books, one half of her body had the skin peeled off, exposing the ligaments, bone and a foetus underneath.

Seeing an exposed skull this early in the morning would have normally seemed quite sinister. But nothing at all at this moment could have made me feel any less excited to be on my way.

Lundy is a small island in the Bristol Channel. Owned and managed by the Landmark Trust, it is three miles long; it has a population of twenty-eight people, and the moment I found out about its existence, I knew I absolutely had to try Door-to-Door Poetry here. By my reckoning, this was the smallest community living in England today.

Lundy was also, as I had recently discovered, a very long way from Newcastle, especially if you're on public transport. It involves a train to London, then another train to Exeter, then a train to Barnstaple, then a bus to Ilfracombe. This journey takes fifteen hours, and that is before you even get on the ferry.

There is a ferry to Lundy every two days and it sets off from the mainland first thing in the morning. There was absolutely no way I could make it there from Newcastle in a day, so I needed to stay overnight in a hotel. This took the total journey time up to eighteen hours, not including the overnight stay. I marvelled at the idea that I could be in China faster than I could be on Lundy Island.

A man in a captain's hat, who I presumed was the captain, announced that we could now board the ferry. He removed a velvet rope that was covering the gangway. Everyone climbed aboard and the engine fired into life, the whole ship juddering and rumbling into action.

As we pulled out of the harbour, I stood on the top deck and gripped the railings as the ship bounced around on the waves. There was something about watching the land fade away, seeing the outline of England getting smaller and smaller, until it lay on the horizon like a fat grey slug. It offered a sense of perspective.

I could feel Lundy pulling me towards it like a big magnet. I could not wait to get started. I kept thinking about how quiet life must be, how mundane the days must seem to the twenty-eight residents who made the place their home. Door-to-Door Poetry would surely be the most exciting thing that had happened on Lundy in a very long time. It was going to blow their minds.

I stepped off the deck into the ship's cabin. I found a seat on a wooden bench and got chatting to a fellow passenger called Roger, a man who'd been coming to Lundy as a volunteer for over twenty years. This week, he told me, he'd be spending his days roaming the fields with a massive flame thrower and setting fire to the rhododendrons.

It turns out rhododendrons are an invasive species. They're a big problem for some of the plants on Lundy. For my part, I couldn't believe playing with a flamethrower was an actual, legitimate job. I told Roger I was feeling quite jealous.

We got chatting about the reasons for my visit.

'Oh you'll love it,' he said. 'It's beautiful. All the people are dead friendly. Apart from the farmer, Kevin, that is. It's best to avoid him really.'

Two hours later, the prehistoric cliffs of Lundy began to swim into focus. Towering geometric cubes of rock got bigger and bigger till they reached far above our heads.

The weather had brightened up, the sun beating down on the turquoise water. We pulled into a small harbour with a concrete slipway. I felt like I'd arrived at the island of Doctor Moreau.

This was the most remote place I'd ever been as a Door-to-Door Poet. There was no phone reception, no internet, no cars. In fact, I'd read that Lundy's entire electricity supply came from an old diesel generator, which is turned off at midnight every night, plunging the whole community into total darkness.

It felt wild, the kind of place where anything could happen. Sort of like *The Wicker Man*. But I was hoping, you know, a bit less burny.

I shuffled off the ferry with the rest of the visitors. We were greeted by a colony of seals, lounging around on the rocks in that self-conscious way that seals always seem to be lounging. It was pupping season, and there were loads of them, all nestled next to their mothers, or taking their first tentative steps into the sea.

I started walking up a winding path that led up the side of a cliff face. I was looking for what I'm going to refer to as the 'town'. It's not really big enough to be a town – it's just where the island's only pub and shop are. I carried on up the winding path, climbing higher and higher up the cliffs. At one point, I paused to catch my breath. I looked down at the harbour below, the ferry now a matchbox miniature, bobbing up and down on a restless sea.

The ground levelled out. I passed through a farmer's

field filled with sheep and horses. I opened a little gate and stepped into a courtyard lined with a cobblestone wall. To my left was the pub, straight in front of me was the shop and to my right was a row of wooden houses.

Having reached what constituted the nearest town, I decided to go for a walk to get my bearings.

It was amazing how few steps you had to take before you were completely and utterly alone. Heading south, I strolled past the ruins of a 13th-century castle. I soon found myself wandering in a moor filled with gorse and heather. I saw an enormous fluffy caterpillar and a very big mushroom. Apart from the bleat of the occasional sheep, it was the quietest place I'd ever been. I felt completely and utterly at peace.

After an hour or so, I turned back and headed towards the 'town'. Going for country walks was all well and good, but it was time to get down to business. I'd already decided I didn't want to write a poem for a tourist while I was here. Instead, I was going to visit the island's shop and see if the staff could recommend a house.

The shop itself stood in the centre of the town, a converted barn with a corrugated iron roof. There was a sign outside that said backpacks were not allowed. Stepping in, there were various aisles cutting across the room like a maze. Despite its minute size, the shop held pretty much every provision you could possibly need. Pasta, cheeses, exotic pickles.

I squeezed up the aisle towards the counter. I spotted a member of staff who looked, unmistakably, like the singer from the Talking Heads, David Byrne.

OK, this was it. It was time to walk up to that cash register and blow the minds of the people of Lundy Island.

I stepped up to David Byrne. I smiled and introduced myself. I explained what I was doing and asked him if he could recommend a house to visit.

I watched as his brow began to furrow.

'Well…' he said, leaning over the counter and looking me straight in the eyes, in a way that seemed to suggest he wanted to make something very clear indeed. 'Most of the staff live in that row of houses over there. But if you came and knocked on my door, I'm not sure I'd feel very *comfortable* with that. There's "No Entry" signs on all of the gates. It's the only place the public aren't supposed to go.'

At this, he smiled. It was a very serious smile.

It struck me that this man was wearing a blue, Landmark Trust t-shirt. There was another member of staff standing next to him, who was also wearing the exact same shirt. Come to think of it, this was the same shirt all the staff were wearing when I got off the ferry too.

It was suddenly very clear to me that all the people who lived on this island worked for the Landmark Trust. That they all worked in the shop, or the pub, or on the ferry. That they all spent every hour of their day serving tourists like me, fetching them things, answering their questions. I don't know why I hadn't thought of this before, but it seemed blatantly obvious now.

I began to panic.

'Look,' David said, as if sensing my growing unease. 'Some of the staff are going to meet up in the pub for a pint tonight. I think the best thing to do is if you come down and try to talk to some of us there. You *might* find someone who's interested.'

I thanked him for his advice and walked quickly back out of the door.

Standing outside the shop, it felt like everything had shifted gears. I could now see how knocking on doors here could be quite intrusive. And I was faced with the possibility that, after this two-day journey, I wouldn't be able to persuade a single resident to get involved.

But there was still one thin sliver of hope. One final thing I could try before I accepted defeat. I was going to have to go to the pub and charm the crap out of the people of Lundy.

And so it came to pass that I found myself outside the Marisco Tavern a few hours later, with the feeling that this entire journey now rested on whatever happened when I stepped through that door.

It was a really lovely pub – the stuff of sea shanties. It was all cobbles, jagged slates and leaded windows. Inside was a mahogany bar with hand-carved furniture. The walls were covered in lifebuoys from ships that had been wrecked off the coast nearby. 'The Halton' from Liverpool, 'The Elan' from Minehead.

To my left, I spotted a group of staff in blue t-shirts, including David Byrne and his colleague from the shop. I took a deep breath and walked over.

This was it. This entire trip, and all of the public money I'd spent trying to get here was riding on this one conversation.

'Hi there. I spoke to this man in the shop earlier. I'm doing an art project and I wondered if you might have a minute and ten seconds to spare?'

'No!' said a man with a thick grey beard.

'Rob!' said the woman next to him, nudging his arm.

'Well, I don't,' Rob said. 'I'm off-shift.'

It was not a strong start.

The woman, who I later found out was Rob's wife, apologised and said that they would hear me out, so long as it was just for one minute. Feeling the pressure, I launched into my introductory poem.

As I rattled through the lines, something quite lovely began to happen. I noticed the staff sit up in their chairs. They were laughing at the bits I hoped they would. David Byrne offered to buy me a pint.

I found a place at the table and we started to introduce ourselves properly. David Byrne was not, in reality, the lead singer of a '70s new wave group. And his name wasn't David, either. It was Ash. His colleague from the shop was called Sue and she was the one who ran the place. Her husband Rob was the island's manager. This information still makes me smile. I had no idea that islands even had managers.

I also met the island's warden, Dean, Helen, who worked in the pub and Barry, who was a property manager.

The group seemed more relaxed. There was a festive atmosphere. I asked them what was important to them and Rob started to talk about life on the island.

'The thing you need to understand is, every day it's something different. Today it's a man going around the country writing poems for people. Tomorrow, it might be the first woman to swim here from the mainland, or a group of stamp enthusiasts, or cloud experts, or the mushroom man – we have a mushroom man. We had a guy who came in and checked all the bottoms of the chairs once. Some of them are hundreds of years old.'

As I listened to Rob, it became clear that there was no way I was ever going to blow the minds of the people of Lundy. To the staff here, I was just another nutter – one in a long line of nutters who arrived like clockwork on the ferry every two days.

In fact, I was to learn that the island had a long, rich history of attracting nutters. There was William de Marisco, who the pub was named after, who fled to Lundy and declared himself king of the island after murdering one of Henry III's messengers. Or William Hudson Heaven, who bought the island in 1834 and created his own currency, 'the puffin', which was intended to replace the pound.

Fifty years to the day before my visit, the Landmark Trust bought the island and turned it into a conservation site. As part of this, the existing residents had been made to stop doing whatever it was they were doing and start working for the company instead.

I was told that these days you could only live on Lundy if you were an employee. Children were not allowed because there was no school, although couples were often hired, presumably because it helped with staff retention.

An hour passed and the table filled up with glasses. It became apparent that there was a subject I could write about here. It was the island. In fact, that's all we seemed to have covered: what the weather was like, how the landscape changed. I suggested a poem about Lundy to the group. They were up for it.

As I got ready to leave, I asked them if there was anyone else they thought might like a poem.

'Well, there's farmer Kevin,' Sue suggested.

This was interesting. I'd been warned about Farmer Kevin. But now he was being recommended instead. It seemed like he might be a tough nut to crack. But I was quite excited by the idea of writing a poem for an actual farmer. There was something kind of Romantic about it. The sort of thing William Blake would definitely have approved of. And I figured, either way, it couldn't hurt to give it a go, could it?

Sue told me that Kevin was around outside the pub most afternoons, that this would be the best way to find him. I thanked her for her help and started to make my goodbyes, before stepping out of the pub on wobbly legs.

You can stay in a house on Lundy but they were all booked up. The only option left was to camp. I didn't mind. I like camping. It would be a nice change of scenery compared to the hotels and sofas I'd been sleeping in and on so far.

I took the short walk over to the campsite. I pitched my tent and crawled inside. I fell asleep that night beneath the stars, the Milky Way lighting up the sky, filling it with colours in a way I never knew it could.

To Lundy

Take me to an island that's three miles long,
where there's only one pub and there's only one shop,
where at twelve every night the power's turned off
and the stars come alive.

Where the sea's chewed by cliffs, sharp as shark's teeth,
where cobblestone ruins are guarded by sheep,
where there's only the roar of the wind on the heath
and no one in sight.

Take me away to this small paradise,
where the turquoise sea blankets the fields on all sides,
and I'll watch as it cradles the coming sunrise,
and I'll sing.

9

LUNDY: PART TWO

I'VE ALWAYS LOVED CAMPING. When I was a kid, my parents used to take me to the Lake District. We'd get the bus to the last stop on the line, wander off into the wilderness and pitch a tent in the middle of some forest, miles from any human habitation.

Years later, I learned this was technically illegal. But we always took our rubbish with us and left everything how we found it. There's worse crimes to have been embroiled in, I suppose.

But if I've learned anything from watching hours of survival documentaries, it's that when you're camping you're always at the mercy of the elements.

So it was when I woke up the next day on Lundy Island, with the unmistakable sensation of the tent ceiling pressing firmly against my face.

As I peeled apart my eyes, I realised a pool of water had been collecting at my feet for quite some time. It had soaked through the sleeping bag and made my lower half feel like it was wrapped in an old sponge. I unzipped the tent and looked outside. I was in the middle of an apocalyptic storm.

I knew the Marisco Tavern opened first thing in the morning. In fact, I'd found out that the place never really closes. Understandably, they don't have a big crime problem on Lundy, owing to the fact that there's not really very far for you to run. Ash told me the pub stops serving at 11pm. But they leave the doors open, just in case anyone is having some kind of emergency. It felt like this would be the perfect time to take them up on that offer.

I ran over to the pub through the wind and the rain. Inside, I ordered a tea and started to weigh up the situation.

I could get through this. There was a ferry the next morning. All I needed to do was find Farmer Kevin, make it through the night and get myself home on the ferry the next day. The wind was battering the tent pretty badly, and it was now leaking, but I was sure I could curl up in a ball and ride this one out, just for one more night.

The barmaid passed me my tea and pointed to a table with some milk and sugar on it. As I picked up the jug, I spotted the island's manager on his way inside.

'It's off,' he said.

'What – the milk?'

'No, the ferry,' he told me. 'There's a big storm coming. There's not going to be any boats off the island for at least a few days.'

My thoughts immediately turned to survival.

'You won't be able to camp,' he added, as if telepathic. 'You're going to have to sleep on the church floor instead.'

In the circumstances, it was a big relief.

'OK,' I told him. 'I was just about to go and find farmer

Kevin. I'll have a word with him first and then move my tent after that.'

'I suggest you move it now,' he replied, soberly. 'It's going to be a big one.'

I arrived back at the campsite shortly after. As if on cue, the weather turned savage. The wind was blowing the rain sideways as it fell in thick drops. The sky cracked with thunder as I pulled the pegs from the ground.

At one point, the door zipped open and the tent filled up with air like a big balloon. It very nearly pulled me off the ground. For a minute, I genuinely thought I was done for. That I would take off in a Monty Python-style comedy of errors, soaring up into the stratosphere, never to be seen again.

I managed to roll everything up into a big ball and drag my stuff through the storm, past the Marisco Tavern, and over to the church at the south end of the island.

St Helena's is a surprisingly massive building. It was commissioned in the 1890s by William Heaven's son, Hudson Grosset Heaven, who spent pretty much every last penny he had on it. It's a big Gothic structure with sinister gargoyles keeping watch from every corner.

In a reflection of our heathen times, St Helena's doesn't get used for praying much these days. It serves mostly as a museum. It is also, as I was to learn, a kind of emergency accommodation too.

I'm not a religious person myself. I can't say I've ever felt particularly excited about churches. But as I reached the arched wooden doorway of St Helena's, I had never been happier to see a house of the Lord. I heaved the door open, dragged my stuff in, and pushed it shut behind me, resting my back against its weight as I let out a deep sigh of relief.

Dripping wet, I plodded into the nave – a cavernous space with stone arches and columns; rows of wooden pews leading up to the altar. Behind this was a huge stained-glass window.

A woman with short grey hair and thick-rimmed glasses appeared, seemingly out of nowhere. This was Vera, the visiting priest.

I explained the situation. She said I'd be welcome to stay.

'I'm sorry I can't offer you a bed,' she added. 'There's only one here and it's mine.'

Instead, Vera showed me a space where I could sleep on the floor, between the organ and the pulpit. Above the organ was a life-sized wooden carving of an eagle, staring back at me with strong Third Reich vibes.

I dragged my stuff across the room and Vera invited me into the kitchen for a cup of tea and a sandwich. The conversation turned to our imminent entrapment.

'I'd better ring my husband,' she said.

This seemed like a good idea. I decided I'd better call Rose, too.

With no mobile phone reception, I walked through the storm to the Marisco Tavern, where there was an old-school payphone in the back corner. I got some change at the bar, stuck a few 20ps in the slot and tapped out Rose's number on the comically chunky keys.

'You're what?' she said.

'I'm trapped on the island. There's a big storm – there's no boats or helicopters or anything.'

'Well when are you going to be back?'

'I'm not really sure.'

'So you're going to miss my family visiting?'

To tell the truth, this had kind of slipped my mind.

'I'm really sorry, Rose, there's nothing I can do. But once I get back, I promise we can—'

The phone went dead.

It was not my finest hour.

I knew this wasn't OK. But there was absolutely nothing I could do about it. I was at the mercy of Poseidon, trapped on Lundy for the foreseeable future. And with no internet, no phone, no TV and no laptop, the only form of entertainment was to sit around and drink beer with the other prisoners on the island. Needless to say, it was a difficult situation, but I threw myself into it with gusto.

In the evening, I had some food at the pub with Vera and we walked back to the church together. I tucked myself into my sleeping bag on the cold stone floor, wrapping up in as many layers as I could find.

I must have drifted off. The next thing I remember was being woken up in the middle of the night by the howling of the wind and a strange, distinctly bestial noise on the other side of the room.

It was a really weird sound, one that I can only describe as 'the chomping of bones'. It was pitch black. At first, I was too scared to even investigate. But the sound didn't seem like it would be going away anytime soon and, after a while,

I decided I'd turn on the lights and find out what it was, just to put my mind at ease.

It was only after I'd got out of the sleeping bag and stumbled in the direction of the light switch that I remembered there was no power, that the island's generator was already off.

I was now standing in total darkness and the sound of the chomping was getting louder. I tried using the torch on my phone, but the church was so big it was like trying to paint a brick wall with a set of watercolours. Out of options, I shuffled back to my sleeping bag. I pulled out some ear plugs and pushed them in as far as they would go. If the stuff of unspeakable nightmares really was going to reach out of the darkness and grab me, at least I wouldn't have to listen to it coming.

When I next woke up, the sun was beaming through the stained-glass windows. It was quiet and bright and incredibly still. Vera came through with a cup of tea and we sat and had some toast in the kitchen. She told me the ferry was still off, but the rain had stopped and the weather had brightened up. I figured I'd start the day with a walk, then see if I could find Farmer Kevin.

I set off up the west side of the island, heading for the northernmost point. It's very exposed to the Atlantic here, and very dramatic-looking. There are huge granite cliffs dropping down towards the sea. Sharp pointy rocks at the bottom, sticking out of the water like jagged teeth. I remember the sheer force of the waves as they broke against those cliffs. The sense of vertigo as I peeked over the side.

I reached the top of the island. It's mostly marshland. There are no buildings, no walls, no signs of human habitation. You can just about make out England to your right. A long way to the left is America.

I ate a sandwich, then walked back to the town along the other side of the island, feeling very lucky to be stuck here.

When I got to the Marisco Tavern, I saw Helen. I asked if she'd seen farmer Kevin. She told me I'd just missed him, that he'd gone home for the day.

I considered giving up on the plan, maybe looking for someone else. But all the signs seemed to be pointing to Kevin.

'I think Kevin would love this,' she said. 'You should definitely ask him.'

'I guess it's probably not a good idea to knock on his door?'

'No, don't do that,' she told me. 'But he's usually outside here at about seven every morning. Why don't you come back then?'

It seemed like a good plan.

I had the rest of the day to kill, so I got a drink and took a seat. I got chatting to a woman called Trysha, who was a rock climber and was here to scale the 'Devil's Slide', a section of cliff said to be particularly challenging and fun, if you're into that sort of thing.

She told me her instructor Ian had recommended it.

'That's funny,' I said. 'I know a rock-climbing instructor called Ian.'

After a few minutes, we realised it was the very same man.

Grantchester is 290 miles from Lundy. England was beginning to feel very small indeed.

I woke up the next day at the crack of dawn. I'd failed in finding Farmer Kevin twice now, and I was sure as hell not going to miss him today. I threw on some clothes and walked over to the Marisco Tavern. I spotted a tractor coming towards me. Inside the cab was a man in green overalls with a white beard. I waved him down.

'Excuse me, are you farmer Kevin?'

'Aye,' he said, in a thick West Country accent.

'I'm going all around the country doing this art project and I wondered if you had a minute and ten seconds to spare?'

'I'm quite busy. Can you give me the gist?'

'Well, basically, I'm writing poems for people on whatever is important to them, but it's not the kind of poetry you might expect.'

He seemed intrigued.

'I'll tell you what,' he said, 'Meet me outside the pub tomorrow at eight in the morning.'

I was meant to be going home the next day. I'd been told the ferries were running again. But the boat was leaving the harbour at midday, which would mean I had plenty of time to chat to Kevin before heading to the port after that. I told Kevin that I'd see him there tomorrow. It was a date.

The next morning, I shoved my stuff in my rucksack and went straight over to the Marisco Tavern. Outside, I spotted Farmer Kevin and gave him a wave. He replied with a nod, then carried on walking into the pub.

OK, I thought. *He's seen me. It's just a matter of time.*

At 08.24 Farmer Kevin came back out of the Marisco Tavern and headed towards the barn. I gave him a wave. He made no reply.

At 09.13 Farmer Kevin went into the pub and came out with a cup of tea. I smiled and waved. He made no reply.

At 09:42 Farmer Kevin drove past me on a red quad bike. I made no movement. He made no reply.

At 10:21 Farmer Kevin drove past the other way. I gave him two thumbs up. He muttered something, but I couldn't hear it over the engine.

At 11:29 I had just over half an hour before I needed to be at the port. I decided the softly softly approach wasn't really working. Farmer Kevin drove past me again, this time with a metal trailer attached to the back of his bike. I waved him down.

'Kevin, are we still on for a chat?'

'I've got to go and pick up some sheep,' he shouted, as he raced past.

'Does that mean we can't talk any more?'

'I've got to go and pick up some sheep,' he shouted again, as if that explained everything perfectly.

And with that, he sped off into the open marsh. Off to do whatever it is a farmer does with his sheep.

Lines Upon Looking for a Shepherd

I went to a field to search for a shepherd,
to seek inspiration to capture in verse,
to ask of a man who's in touch with the land
what secrets he'd learned while he nurtured the earth.

He smiled and said he was attending his flock
but offered to meet me around eight o'clock
the next day, by the tavern, it sounded like heaven.
I asked for his name and he told me it: Kevin.

O Kevin, O Kevin, where did I go wrong?
I stood by the pub in the wind and the rain.
O Kevin, why did you turn down my sweet song?
I waited for hours and you never came.

I ran to the meadows, to where the cows graze,
I ran to the barn, to where the hens lay,
I ran to the church, they said *We've never met him,*
I stood on the hilltops and shouted out, Kevin!

O Kevin, O Kevin, are you still alive?
What can I do to ensnare you with art?
O Kevin, I can't get you out of my mind,
I must know the innermost depths of your heart.

I could pen lines while you shear the lamb's fleeces,
I'll help feed the pigs, I'll pick up their faeces,
just come to me Kevin, I swear it's not weird,
all I want is to bury my face in your beard!

It's my only desire, I won't stop till I find you,
I'll roam round these hills till the last bells of time
pursuing the shadows of flat caps and denim,
as the wind howls and taunts me with whispers of Kevin.

10

LIMERICK – A BRIEF DIVERSION

I WAS TRAPPED ON LUNDY for a total of five days. Arriving back on the mainland was a bit like the final scenes of *Cast Away*. I'd got quite used to being stranded, the slow pace of life, the certainty. It took a little while to readjust to the modern world – to things like traffic lights and chewing gum and big crowds. And that was just in Ilfracombe harbour.

I got off the ferry and hopped straight on the bus home. I waved goodbye to Vera through the window as I pulled out of the station. It felt like we'd been a part of something.

In many ways, Lundy wasn't really what I was expecting. Neither North nor South, but somewhere off to the West. It had been a surprise to get stuck there for starters. But despite being stranded, I'd found the whole place to be a peculiarly 21st-century experience – the fact that the island had a manager, that everyone had to wear a uniform.

Don't get me wrong, I'd really enjoyed my time there. I'd happily go on holiday to Lundy any day of the week. But as I mulled it all over on the long trip back to Newcastle, I couldn't shake the feeling that the place was all very controlled as well. In the way that most natural places in England are controlled, I suppose.

The other thing I couldn't help but notice about Lundy was that it was…well… Lundy was quite middle-class. And hey, look. There's nothing wrong with that. I'm not being classist or anything. I promise. Some of my best friends are middle-class.

But I'd been thinking it might be fitting if this trip could capture a snapshot of the land I live in, a record of the people living in it. And no matter how pretty it was, Lundy didn't seem to be representing what I think of when I think of England. I'd decided I needed a change of direction.

Before I did any of this, however, I really needed to try and smooth things over with Rose. The results weren't exactly immediate.

She'd said it was fine, that there would be other chances to spend time with her family. But I knew this wasn't really good enough. It definitely needed fixing.

Something had to be done. The first and most obvious solution being that I should probably spend a bit more time around the house.

And that was the plan. Really it was. But fate seemed to be pulling me elsewhere. Because while I was swanning about on Lundy, taking pictures of baby seals and massive caterpillars, something quite interesting had happened at home, and it had begun to seem like an opportunity I couldn't really afford to pass up on.

When I got back, I found out my grandparents had been doing a bit of family history. They'd discovered that the

McCabes originally came from Ireland.

They couldn't dig up any information on where in Ireland we were from, or how we might have arrived in the North-East. But they did find out that we have a family motto. And it's pretty savage as well: 'Either to conquer or to die'.

This is a cut-throat and brutal statement, isn't it? But the McCabes were mercenaries in the 14th century, so I suppose that's the kind of code you'd very much want to live your life by. Though I'm not sure their old saying is so much in keeping with my relatively sheltered 21st-century lifestyle. The only time it might have seemed appropriate is during the occasional game of Monopoly, or while playing with conkers on the school playground. 'Conker or die' would be more fitting for me, really.

Either way, finding out my family came from Ireland did plant an interesting seed in my head.

My grandparents hadn't been able to figure out exactly where the McCabes came to England from. I had a look myself – I couldn't find anything either. But I was thinking it might still be fun to try Door-to-Door Poetry over there. I'd never been to Ireland before. It would be nice to have a look around.

Granted, I'd been sticking pretty closely to England so far on this adventure. But that didn't really matter, did it?

And I'd started wondering, if I couldn't travel to the place the McCabes originally hailed from, maybe I could choose somewhere else in Ireland instead.

As I sat at my desk, I began to ask myself what the most poetical-sounding place in Ireland might be. And you don't have to spend very long on Google before you realise where it is. Because the most poetical-sounding place in Ireland is, quite obviously, the city of Limerick.

I love a good limerick. I imagine there are people out there who don't think limericks are proper poetry. I think they're wrong. Limericks are one of the finest forms of poetry. A poem that you can show to a member of the general public without them recoiling in horror is a special thing. The limerick holds that power. I like the fact that they're often rude. I like that they usually have a magical element to them, but that the magic causes a hilarious and unexpected side-effect.

Consider the story of the man from Madras:

There was a young man from Madras,
his balls they were made out of brass.
In wintery weather
he'd knock them together
and sparks would fly out of his ass.

What's not to love?

A trip to Limerick was beginning to feel really important. It would be exciting to try Door-to-Door Poetry in another country. It would be interesting to travel to the spiritual home of the limerick, too. How might this influence the kind of responses I got? I wanted to know the answer.

But it wasn't as if I had to travel to Limerick right away. After all, I could go there any time I wanted. There was no rush. And there was definitely no need to shoot off again as soon as I got home, especially after being trapped on Lundy

Island for five days.

This is exactly what I would have been thinking, if it wasn't for one small problem: Limerick, as it happens, is quite far away. Even further than Lundy. And I was starting to run out of money.

On account of this, I'd found myself casually scrolling through the website of a popular budget airline, just to see how possible such a trip might actually be. As I did, I'd discovered there was one very cheap option that would get me to Limerick for a fraction of the average cost.

It would involve a train, a flight and two coaches. But it would get me there on an absolute shoestring. The only catch was that I'd need to set off in a few weeks' time.

This was too much, wasn't it? Surely, I couldn't justify travelling all that way, to a town I knew nothing about, just because a rude kind of poem was named after it?

And yet, though I know it sounds a bit crazy, I'd come to believe this was the only logical way of moving this project forward.

Needless to say, when I told Rose about the idea, she was not exactly overjoyed.

'But why do you have to go now?' she asked.

'Because the flights are incredibly cheap,' I explained.

At this, she let out a sigh of exasperation. I was not the most popular member of our household.

In the end, Rose gave the trip her blessing, so long as I promised to tell her as soon as I'd booked the tickets, so she could invite her mother to come and keep her company.

And though I know it's probably quite hard to understand,

I'd decided that this was really worth doing. No matter how silly my motivation for going, something seemed to be pulling me in the direction of Limerick.

On the 4th of October I took the train over to Manchester. I spent the night at my friend Bee's house before heading to the airport the following day. On my way, the taxi driver asked if I was going on holiday. I filled him in on the story.

'Poetry?' he said. 'Will it not be a bit boring?'

I told him I was hoping it wouldn't be.

The flight was at 6am. The sun was just beginning to rise as I arrived at the airport. As I walked through the sliding glass doors, briefcase in hand, it was becoming very apparent just what kind of a commitment I had really made here.

This wasn't a case of hopping on a train or a ferry any more. I needed to pass through customs. There were machines, security guards. People wanted to check my bags and, in my case, my right boot, which one member of the border force was very keen to make sure wasn't concealing anything it shouldn't be.

When I'd booked the tickets online, I'd been asked what the purpose of my trip was. How do you even answer that kind of question? I had a purpose – this much I knew. But it was quite a specific one. A cause that seemed beyond the parameters of a thirty-character box.

I'd also begun to feel a bit worried about what was going to happen when I arrived. About whether I'd be able to make the whole thing work.

By now, I was getting a bit of a handle on the way the English were taking to Door-to-Door Poetry. I would describe their responses as 'polite and fairly receptive'. When it came to the Irish, however, all bets were off.

It felt like it could go either way. On the one hand, the Irish people were renowned for being friendly. They had a long history of supporting poets. They'd produced many fine ones.

On the other, I'd begun to wonder if the fact that I was English might not exactly work to my advantage here. I was feeling nervous about the logo on my jacket. After I'd set off, I'd noticed that the overcoat I'd brought was embossed with a mod-style target, which itself is based on the logo of the British Royal Air Force. Perhaps not the best statement to be making in the Irish Republic...

The flight from Manchester to Belfast was extremely short. It was so short that the captain introducing himself at the start of the journey seemed like more of an afterthought, as opposed to something that was actually necessary.

'The weather in Belfast today is pretty much the same as it is here,' he'd said, as if deliberately stating the obvious.

We descended into Belfast forty minutes later. I caught a coach to Dublin and we crossed the border. The driver of this coach had a penchant for vintage club classics, meaning the entire journey was soundtracked by the likes of 'Rhythm Is A Dancer' and 'Touch Me' by Rui Da Silva.

I changed coaches in Dublin. On the way, I passed the Guinness Brewery, which looked every bit like the drunken Willy Wonka's factory I imagined it would. By the middle of the afternoon, I'd arrived safe and sound in Limerick.

My first impressions were that I liked Limerick. The bus

dropped us at Arthur's Quay Park in the city centre. There were bollards painted brightly with different characters faces on, making them look like Vikings or mermaids.

At a nearby supermarket, I stopped to get a sandwich and some fruit, but was confused about which products were available in the meal-deal offer. Not one, but two members of staff came to my assistance, going over to the shelves to fetch the whole range of items I was entitled to, before holding them up for my close inspection. In the process, one of them asked what I was doing in Limerick.

'Maybe you could write a poem about how nice the staff are?'

I told her I would keep it in mind.

It was getting a bit late in the day to start knocking. I decided I would check my bags in at the nearby hostel, then take a walk around town.

I wandered through cobbled streets, past the Gallery of Art and the Hunt Museum. I took a stroll along the River Shannon, which was much wider and grander than I'd imagined it would be.

Little white sailing boats were moored along the sides. I passed a couple having an earnest conversation on a park bench and a young man selling bucket hats with the town's coat of arms on.

Having had a good wander, I decided it would be nice to sample a Guiness. It also felt like the right time to quiz a few people in Limerick, too. I wanted to ask them if they had a favourite limerick, to get a measure of the poetic competition before I got started.

To this end, I found myself in a pub called Micky Martin's, which was down a back alley just off Thomas Street. The archway above the door was bright pink, the door itself made of Mackintosh stained glass.

As I sipped on the aforementioned stout, I turned to two young men who were sitting at the table next to me.

'Excuse me lads, I was wondering if you have a favourite limerick?'

'You mean, like, a favourite place to visit?' said one.

'No, I mean, as in the kind of poem. Do you have a favourite limerick?'

They both looked at me blankly.

'You know,' I said. '"There once was a man from Nantucket…"'

'Are you looking for somewhere to eat?' said the second lad.

'No. Forget about Limerick the place,' I said. 'I mean the kind of poem – a limerick.'

I pulled up a list of limericks on my phone. I started to share some.

'I don't understand how those are different to any other poem,' said the first lad.

'Well, they always follow the same pattern,' I explained. 'And they're usually rude.'

There was an awkward silence.

After a few minutes, I found out that the two of them were actually from Poland and Latvia. So I suppose that would explain the confusion. What seemed baffling to me was that they'd lived in Limerick for eleven and nineteen years respectively and had never once heard that the town was also the name of a poem. I couldn't believe no one had mentioned this before.

Keen to conduct more research, I left the pub and walked down the street. I stopped an older couple who were waiting at some traffic lights.

'Do you live in Limerick?' I asked.

'Yes,' they both said.

'Do either of you have a favourite limerick?'

'No.'

'OK. It's just, I'm here visiting from Newcastle and I've chosen to come mostly because the name of this place is also the name of a poem. I was wondering if people here ever tell each other any limericks at all?'

'Not really,' said the man.

I think he could tell I felt a bit deflated.

'You see that white pub across the road?' he said. 'There's some limericks hung on the wall in there. Why don't you have a look?'

I thanked them both and crossed the street.

I searched for the limericks inside the pub, but they were nowhere to be seen. At the bar, I asked the person serving if she knew anything about them.

'Haven't a clue,' she said.

I asked her if she had heard of a limerick before.

'I have a masters in English literature,' she told me. 'So yes, I have.'

'Do you have a favourite limerick?' I enquired.

'Not really, no.'

I thanked her anyway and left, making my way back to the hostel.

Finding a limerick in the town of Limerick was proving a little harder than I'd expected. Maybe the people here just wanted to leave the limerick behind them. Maybe it was a bit old-fashioned.

But as I walked out of the city centre that evening, I simply couldn't accept this. Surely the limerick wasn't dying, was it? In the very place it should be most ubiquitously known and celebrated. What if the people of Limerick had just forgotten how great limericks really were?

With this conundrum still very much on my mind, I woke up the next day in the hostel and headed out to knock on some doors.

I had chosen a street not too far from where I was staying. Lord Edward Street. It was a mixture of all different kinds of houses, three-bedroom semis, newbuild flats, cobblestone cottages. Right at the top of the road was a row of terraced bungalows, the fronts painted in a creamy white.

I took a deep breath and opened the black metal gate of the first bungalow. I walked up the paved drive and tapped on the letterbox.

After a minute, a middle-aged man answered in a chequered shirt and glasses. His arm was in a sling.

I showed him my introductory poem and he told me his name was Patrick. I asked Patrick what was important to him.

'I used to be a campanologist,' he said.

'What's a campanologist?'

'It's the official term for a bell-ringer. I studied the design and tuning of bells, and also the different ways you can ring them.'

'I see. Can I ask you one more question, Patrick?'

He told me I could.

'Do you have a favourite limerick?'

A Limerick for the Limerick-starved Citizens of Limerick

There was a young man called Seamus,
who ate a whole church, and got famous.
When he'd drunk enough wine
his burps told the time
and wedding bells came from his anus.

11

BIRMINGHAM

WHEN I SET OFF FOR IRELAND, I was keen to avoid any shameful stereotypes. With this in mind, it seemed a little ironic that the first person who answered the door was called Patrick, that he was a church bell-ringer, and that he was objectively the most quintessentially Irish man you could have possibly come across.

For balance, I just want to add that I spoke to two other people that day. There was James, who asked for a poem about an alternative hip-hop artist, and there was Bilal, who asked for one about the importance of being kind to others.

I couldn't turn either of these subjects into a good limerick though. And it's my book. If I want to subject you to a flippant poem about church bells coming from someone's rectum, then I can. There's nothing you can do about it.

Still, my conversations with Patrick, James and Bilal did raise an important point. All in all, I'd had a really lovely time in Ireland. But there's only so much you can glean from a country after a couple of passing visits. After delivering the poems, I flew back to Newcastle. It had begun to feel like I was stepping into something I wasn't quite ready for.

This journey had started because a posh-sounding woman had told me that Door-to-Door Poetry would never work with anyone outside the North-East of England. And I was beginning to feel like I hadn't quite finished what I'd set out to do. I was also feeling like I wanted to try something a little bit different as well.

So far on this journey, I'd been meeting people by knocking on their doors at random. Not that there's anything wrong with that. This is exactly what a Door-to-Door Poet should be doing, by my reckoning.

But I'd been thinking about my time with the residents of Lundy. About how I'd met them in the local pub. It wasn't technically their home, but Ash had told me that the pub, for the residents of Lundy, was pretty much like their living room. It was where they went to relax, where all their post got delivered.

It had got me thinking about the different places people might call home. It struck me that there were a lot of individuals out there who didn't have a door for me to knock on in the first place. And I was feeling that if I really wanted to meet as many different people as possible, it was time to find a way to reach out to them too.

It was now the 17th of November, 08:02 am, and I was sitting on a train, speeding towards Birmingham.

Earlier that month, I'd spoken to my friend Ben. He'd passed me an email for an organisation called St Basil's. St Basil's is a charity that offers accommodation to young people who have become homeless.

I'd arranged a phone call with a man called Azim – an

executive who told me that he'd worked for St Basil's for the past sixteen years. This seemed like a pretty good vote of confidence.

I explained to Azim what I'd been up to and he invited me along to one of their provisions in the south of the city.

Like Limerick, Birmingham was a city I'd never been to before. Unlike Limerick, however, Birmingham was a very busy place to encounter on a weekday afternoon. At least on the day I arrived, anyway. People were flying in every direction as I fought my way through New Street Station. I've never seen so many bodies moving so fast.

As I wove between hordes of travellers shooting off to their various platforms, I could make out snippets of conversations. For some inexplicable reason, I found myself feeling a profound affinity with Brummies.

I had never had this feeling before. I haven't had it since. I had no evidence to support the feeling, apart from the choice bits of conversation I heard. But there was something in the way people spoke that day – an openness, a friendliness, an effort not to take yourself too seriously. It reminded me of home.

The other thing that made a strong first impression was how many unusual buildings I passed as soon as I left the station. There's a load of buildings in Birmingham that could quite easily be leftover scenery from the set of a Stanley Kubrick film. I'm thinking of The Selfridges shopping centre in particular, looking, as it does, like a spacecraft from an episode of *Doctor Who*.

I peered up at the thousands of metal discs that make up

its shell, a space-aged tube ferrying pedestrians backwards and forwards from the car park. I would not have been the slightest bit surprised if it had closed itself off and taken flight right there in the street, shooting back to whichever galaxy it originally hailed from.

Oddly, as I walked over to the B&B, Birmingham's architecture seemed to move further and further back in time. In fact, once I'd got to the hotel itself, we appeared to have travelled backwards by about four hundred years. The building was an original Elizabethan tavern, complete with half-timbered walls. The hallways were tiny, the ceilings low – owing to the fact that everyone was so miniature in the olden days.

As a member of staff showed me up the stairs, I found out that Queen Elizabeth I had actually once slept in the room I was in, which was a nice surprise. Whatever your views on the monarchy, it's always a good sign of quality when a queen has scoped out your digs ahead of you.

Birmingham had done a lot to impress me so far. But finding out I was staying in the same room as a monarch did leave me feeling a little self-conscious, especially when I considered the purpose of my trip.

There was surely no starker contrast in privilege than leaving a Tudor queen's bedroom, before heading over to a provision for those who are experiencing homelessness. But there wasn't much that could be done about that now. Instead, I grabbed my briefcase, stepped out of the B&B and set off for St Basil's.

I walked down a busy motorway, crossed a road, went

through an alley with a number of closed-down shops in it, then crossed another motorway. I passed into a council estate in a quiet suburb.

I spotted a modern, shiny two-storey complex, plonked conspicuously at the end of a newly built cul-de-sac. This, I assumed, must be the place.

I walked up the path to a red metal door. I pressed the intercom. I waited. I waited for quite some time. Nobody answered.

I pressed the button again, wondering whether this was really the right place after all. In fact, I was about to walk away and try somewhere else when a lady with braided hair and a lanyard came out.

'Hi. Come in,' she said. 'Sorry it took a little while. You're at the wrong door.'

We passed through the reception and took a sharp left into a bustling office with lots of desks and people making calls at them. I was greeted by Azim, a man in a blue England rugby shirt with a very infectious smile. He shook my hand, made me a cup of tea, then took me on a tour of the place.

St Basil's was a calm and tidy building. There was a lot of space, an occasional potted plant. It felt more like the hub of some graphic design business than somewhere you might actually live.

We started the tour in the communal living area – a room painted bright turquoise, with a series of coffee tables and an Ikea sofa. Four young people were sitting in there as we passed through. They each gave me a little wave.

To give him his dues, Azim was a really attentive guide.

You could tell he took a lot of pride in what he did. He told me that St Basil's was a charity that offered accommodation to young people who had nowhere else to go. This building was for male and female residents. It had twenty-five bedrooms. It was what they classed 'emergency accommodation', which meant that young people could live here for up to three months. After this, they would be re-located to more permanent housing.

Azim told me that they were keen to do more than just offer a place to stay. They ran training and education courses, as well as counselling and therapy sessions. It seemed like a tightly run ship. And I noticed that everyone I passed along the way – whether they were staff or the young people themselves – looked bright-eyed and happy to be there.

Azim led me up a winding staircase into an IT suite. In the centre was a circular table with chairs. We each found a seat and started to go over the plan.

We agreed it wasn't really a good idea to go around knocking on doors here. These young people had already had enough unexpected surprises. Instead, Azim suggested that the young people come up and see me, one at a time. He told me that he'd already suggested this to a number of the residents, that they'd all sounded really enthusiastic about it.

The idea of anyone sounding enthusiastic about poetry was a nice vote of confidence. It felt like a welcome change.

Azim left the room and went to fetch the first person of the day. Soon after, a lad in his early twenties came in. He had baggy jeans, a white hoodie and short cropped hair with lines shaved neatly into the sides. He had a playful look in his eyes – the look of someone who seemed to understand exactly how silly all of this really was. Make of that what you will.

I shook his hand and he told me his name was Ibrahim. I asked Ibrahim if he knew what I was there for. He told me he'd heard a bit about it, but he wasn't a hundred per cent sure. I decided to start at the beginning.

I showed him my introductory poem. I told him that, normally, I would do this after knocking on a door. I asked him to try and imagine that.

Once I'd finished, I asked what was important to him.

Ibrahim told me he was training to be a PE teacher. He already had some qualifications in sports psychology. Having passed the initial course, he was set to start his teacher training in the next academic year. He told me he was really looking forward to it.

Truth be told, my understanding of physical education is pretty basic. I was a rotund child. I was often picked last in sporting activities. In fact, the only positive feedback I ever received in PE was that I was a 'good sport'. Undoubtedly a very positive attribute. But let's face it, it's not exactly the kind of thing that's going to get you onto team GB.

In an attempt to get deeper into the psyche of a physical educationalist, I asked Ibrahim what inspired him about the subject.

'You're helping people,' he said. 'You can help them with the physical side, but you can also improve their mental health as well. A few of my friends were never really into sports. Now I've encouraged them to start, they're more energetic, more "out there".'

I have to say, Ibrahim was making a pretty convincing argument. And listening to him that day, it occurred to me that none of my PE teachers had ever really talked about the purpose of what we were doing, or the benefits it might have. It seemed to me that if they had spent a bit more time explaining why we were being forced to do laps around the field in the pouring rain, it might have made it all seem a bit less traumatic.

As a stereotypical lazy artist, I told Ibrahim I tended to do as little moving around as possible. I asked him if he could recommend a sport for me to try, a good place to get started.

'Football,' he said, laughing. 'It doesn't really feel like exercise.'

I thanked him for the tip.

It had been lovely chatting to him. And I felt sure Ibrahim was going to make a really brilliant teacher. He'd already gone a long way towards changing my mind. Not wanting to take up too much of his time, I thanked him for getting involved and left him to get back to his day.

As he shut the door behind him, I couldn't help but wonder what had led such a friendly and intelligent young man as Ibrahim to end up in a place like this. I would have liked to know more. But I was pleased not to have forced the conversation in that direction either, to have given Ibrahim the chance to talk about whatever was important to him. If nothing else, his story seemed to be a stark reminder that we should never judge a book by its cover.

As soon as he left, there was a tap at the door. Azim went out, then quickly came back in again.

'You have some visitors, Rowan.'

It seemed that word about my arrival had spread. A group of eighteen-year-olds were now gathered outside, all eagerly awaiting their own Door-to-Door Poetry poem. It was heartwarming. And I smiled at the fact that, for the first time on this adventure, someone else was doing the knocking.

We decided to invite the whole group in at once. A few seconds later, the four of them filed in: first Morgan, a girl with a stripy yellow jumper and thick-rimmed glasses; then a girl called Nagr in a black hijab and a green bomber jacket; then a boy in a blue hoodie called Chappo and, finally, Naya. Naya had really long, straight black hair and a very cool pair of white trainers on.

Within a few minutes, our conversation had turned to the upcoming general election. Morgan told us that she wished she knew a little bit more about the different parties – about what they stood for. I asked the group if they felt like this was something that was missing from their education, something they would have liked to be taught more about.

'That's not what education is for though,' Naya argued. 'The education system is designed to get people working in factories. That's why everyone is given rules. That's why everyone sits in a row and has to put their hand up. And that's why social and racial inequality is inevitable.'

In terms of conversation starters, we had somewhat dived in at the deep end.

Naya's thoughts on education stood in stark contrast to the conversation I'd just had with Ibrahim. It got me thinking about the kinds of reasons someone might get into teaching in the first place, about the wrongs they might be yearning to right.

We started to talk about inequality, about how young people often seem to draw the shortest straw.

'People our age aren't going to be able to afford a flat, never mind a house,' Naya said. 'The value of the pound is going down, Uni prices are going up. Everyone deserves a chance to be at their happiest, but there are young people out there who are struggling to get by.'

Morgan, Nagr and Chappo all nodded in agreement. It was clearly a subject that was close to their hearts.

I showed the group my introductory poem. When I got to the end, I asked them what was important to them. Naya spoke up first, pretty much immediately.

'I think sixteen-year-olds should have the vote,' she said.

Second Class

I never understood the logic
when I was sixteen years old.
If I worked, I'd pay my taxes,
but I didn't get to vote.

I could join the Royal Air Force,
they might teach me how to fly,
but I didn't get to choose
who sent me off to die.

I could get married, have a kid,
move into my own place,
get drunk in a restaurant
and even change my name.

But to put a little pencil cross
in a flimsy paper box
was beyond all possibility,
I was not mature enough.

As if everyone over eighteen
was politically zen,
as if they hadn't made a mess of it
when it was left to them.

Like worker's rights, the price of rent,
were just none of my business,
when there were older voters
who wouldn't even feel the difference.

And I wondered then, as I do now,
is it part of our leader's plan?
Are they scared of how the vote would go
when placed in younger hands?

Do they know they wouldn't last
in power for a minute,
if they dragged the past out of the booth
and placed the future in it.

12

ST GEMMA'S HOSPICE

It was now the 9th of December. It was three days before the general election and I was peering through a set of metal gates outside a hospice in Leeds.

Across the car park stood a tall, yellow brick building. There were two ambulances parked next to it. Visitors were coming and going through the automatic doors. Just above them was a giant statue of Jesus. He was wearing what appeared to be a fantastically huge wrestling cape, his hands out to the side as if he were saying *Come and have a go, if you think you're hard enough.*

The statue itself was suspended on the wall, making it look like Jesus was hovering in mid-air above the bustle of activity below. I went to take a picture, then stopped halfway through. There were a lot of patients around. Was it disrespectful to be taking pictures of the giant wrestler Jesus? I put my camera back in my pocket and decided to err on the side of caution.

I'd now written poems for twenty-one people. I only had nine more to go before I reached my self-imposed target of thirty.

By this point, the ongoing excitement of it all was beginning to take its toll.

I'd been knocking on doors for the best part of a year. I was beginning to lose track of the amount of hotel rooms I'd spent the night in, how many vegetable dhansaks I'd ordered. And as the project ran its course, I was beginning to notice quite a big contradiction in what I was trying to do.

This adventure was supposed to be about getting closer to strangers – about connection. But I'd begun to appreciate the profound irony of the fact that I was spending more time on my own than at any other time in my life.

The trip back to Birmingham felt particularly lonely. The evening before I delivered the poems, I ate a sad dhansak in a restaurant called Manzils. Aside from showing my ticket to an inspector and ordering some poppadoms, I hadn't had a meaningful conversation with another human being in quite some time.

Something didn't feel right. I thought about how many birthday parties I'd flaked out on, how many wedding invitations I'd had to turn down. I hadn't really expected this to happen so often.

But there was no way of slowing down. It seemed like, whatever I did next, I needed to keep moving towards the finishing line.

I'd been feeling a little bit stuck after Birmingham. I wasn't exactly sure where to go next. I'd enjoyed my visit to St Basil's. It had been interesting to think about the different places someone might call home. I wanted the next location to be doing something similar to that. But I had no idea where that kind of place might be.

Imagine my surprise, then, when I opened up my laptop and discovered an email from a woman called Clare. Clare's real, actual job title was 'The Head of Transformation', which seemed like the exact person I needed to speak to at that particular moment.

Clare explained that she worked for a charity called St Gemma's. St Gemma's offered free healthcare to people who were approaching the end of their life. I learned that this is sometimes called 'palliative care'.

Clare told me she'd heard about my project and was wondering if I'd be interested in meeting some of her patients. It seemed like a great idea.

That was, until I gave it a little more thought.

On the one hand, it would definitely be refreshing to have a place chosen for me for once. I was struggling a bit with the planning. And I think it's worth stressing again here how crap I am at geography. My main method for choosing locations had been to stick a pin in a cartoon map and then google areas of interest nearby. It was a method that had, quite often, led to some very interesting encounters. But there's only so many times you can stick a pin in a cartoon map before you become a little overwhelmed by the meaninglessness of it all. Hovering as I was on the verge of some kind of existential crisis, Clare's email had felt like a welcome sense of direction.

But the excitement of the invitation had soon given way to the cold, hard reality of it all. I had never worked in a hospice. I had no formal training in this field. What if I did something to upset someone? I didn't want these patients to feel pressured into talking about their personal lives. I didn't want them to feel like I was exploiting anyone's misery.

After a bit of positive encouragement from Clare, I'd decided to take her up on her offer. I felt there must be a way of making this work. And, morbid as it sounded, Clare had assured me that the people I would be meeting at St Gemma's really wouldn't have very long left to live – I couldn't help but wonder how this might affect the kinds of things they spoke about.

I'd been standing at the iron gates for what seemed like a very long time now. I felt extremely out of my comfort zone. I had tried to tell myself this was understandable. It was, after all, the entire point of the visit. But I was still finding it difficult to get my head around the fact that the people I met today would be dead in the not-too-distant future. It felt weird to admit this to myself. As if, by doing it, I was being overly pessimistic; as if I was giving up the hope I should be holding out for them.

I pulled myself away from the fence and stepped uncertainly into the hospice. I walked to the main entrance and explained to the receptionist what I was there for. I then found a seat near the gift shop, next to a wall of various knick-knacks: gnomes, miniature snow-globes.

A few minutes later, a woman called Heather came over in a nurse's uniform. She invited me upstairs to her office. I found out on the walk up there that Heather was, in fact, the chief nurse here at St Gemma's. I hadn't realised my visit had been so keenly anticipated.

As we walked through the halls, Heather told me she'd been intrigued when she first heard about the project, that she was looking forward to seeing what I came up with. After this, we started to talk about the Happy Mondays.

Heather was, like me, a big fan of the band, and was currently lamenting the fact that she'd missed a reunion gig in the city centre. It seemed a strange conversation to be having in light of what we were doing, but it helped to settle my nerves in a funny sort of way.

We sat down in a room covered in wood panelling. We started to go over the plan. Heather explained that a lot of the patients here had quite a lot on their plates. Understandably, some of them might not want to be bothered by this kind of thing. So her idea was that I would follow one of the nurses around on the ward. This nurse would go into each patient's room and explain what I was doing. If the patient was up for getting involved, I could go in and speak to them as normal. It sounded like a good idea.

At this point, the nurse in question, Amanda, walked in.

'Right,' she said. 'Should we get started?'

It felt abrupt. Unceremonious, even. But then, what was I expecting would happen here? These were busy people. They had work to do. It was time to get moving.

Amanda led me down a flight of stairs and on to the first ward. There were white walls, pine skirting boards, a strong smell of disinfectant. In the distance, I could hear the faint beeping of life-support machines.

I was asked to sanitise my hands and keep my sleeves rolled up at all times. Having sterilised myself, I sat down

143

on a chair in the hallway while Amanda went into the first patient's room. Doctors and nurses rushed past in their scrubs, wheeling equipment on trolleys, speaking in a technical jargon I would never understand.

It felt strange sending Amanda ahead of me, like some kind of poetry canary. I began to muse on how much easier the whole trip would have been if I could have sent someone in advance. Maybe one day, I thought, I'd be able to outsource all of the work. Like Andy Warhol. There'd be someone to pick the location, someone to knock, someone to write the poems.

I was interrupted from these egotistical musings by the sound of Amanda's voice. She told me that we had a yes. I stood up and followed her slowly inside.

It was a spacious room with a hospital bed, a dining table and a balcony. Sat in an armchair was a man in his eighties with big brown eyes. He was wearing a white checked shirt, his hair thinning on top.

'Lewis, this is Rowan,' Amanda said. 'I'll leave you both to get on with it.'

I said hello and pulled up a chair next to Lewis. I remember feeling a little shocked by how thin he looked, the ramifications of where I was and what I was doing now fully sinking in. I showed him my introductory poem.

'I used to read quite a lot of poetry when I was young,' Lewis told me, in a soft Yorkshire accent. He went on to quote a section from a poem I later found out was called 'The Loss of the Birkenhead' by Francis Hastings Charles Doyle.

'*Right on our flank the crimson sun went down, the deep sea rolled around in dark repose...*'

The fact he could still remember all this from his school days impressed me no end.

There followed what you might call a 'period of adjustment'. It took us a little while to settle into a relaxed conversation. It struck me that my role in Lewis' room was, as yet, not really very clearly defined. I wasn't a friend or a family member; I wasn't a doctor or a nurse; I wasn't a journalist, or an entertainer. I sensed Lewis was trying to figure out what I was about and how much I needed to know for it to work. Unspoken questions seemed to float around in the space above our heads. As if to help diffuse these, Lewis started to explain his illness.

'The doctors had a good idea of what it was. I should have seen someone much sooner. It was my daughter who rang them. The specialist told me I had prostate cancer, that it had spread to my kidneys.'

'The thing that worries me the most is thinking about what's going to happen to my wife,' he said. 'She has dementia and she needs someone to look after her.'

Lewis told me he'd been trying very hard to get his wife into a care home, but it was just too expensive. He seemed frustrated by this. Having, he said, worked hard and been careful with money his whole life, he didn't think he should have to be in this situation. There was talk of his wife perhaps being able to stay with his son, who lived in Cumbria.

'He's got a beautiful garden,' Lewis said. 'There's lots of squirrels there.'

I found it surprising to learn that, when it came to the idea of his own death, Lewis was pretty stoic.

'I'm not worried about what happens next,' he told me. 'I'm eighty-five for Christ's sake! I don't believe in an afterlife.'

I asked him where he thought these beliefs – or lack of them – had come from.

'I went to a church school. It was a terrible place. Just after my mother died, I was sat listening to this vicar. I thought to myself, *what a load of rubbish*. From then on, the more I listened, the dafter it seemed.'

Playing devil's advocate, I asked him if the idea of a god or heaven could give you something to hope for, something to believe in.

'People should believe in themselves,' he replied. 'When I was twelve, me and my pal went into a spiritualist meeting. The spiritualist came on and said, "I'm getting a message from someone whose name begins with W." This woman put her hand up and said, "It's my husband, Walter – he's recently passed." The spiritualist said, "Walter is telling me that he likes the new fireplace…"

'Well pretty soon, me and my friend, we both start laughing. This feller came to throw us out. He asked why we were laughing and I said, "It doesn't make any sense. Walter is supposed to be in heaven. He's got everything he could ever want. And all he can think to do is come back and talk about a new bloody fireplace."'

I admired Lewis for his humour in the face of adversity. It felt we'd hit on some common ground. A nurse came in with some soup and a can of coke and this seemed like the right time to leave. I thanked him for getting involved and left him to eat his food in peace.

Outside, Amanda led me a little further down the hall. I waited at the door of another room before she came out and gave me the thumbs up. This time, I met a man called Murray. He was lying on his bed in blue-striped pyjamas.

'You're a poet,' he said to me with a wry smile. 'But do you know it?'

Murray told me he was a big fan of Spike Milligan. Him and his wife loved music hall. They used to go down to Leeds City Varieties quite regularly, a large old venue in the city centre where they still film *The Good Old Days*.

We spoke about the difference between an old-fashioned variety show and a modern one.

'They had acrobats and comedians, poets – all sorts,' Murray told me. 'Everyone would join in the songs. The audience were very critical too. They used to boo if they didn't like it.'

I suggested a poem about the Leeds City Varieties. He seemed up for it. At this point, a nurse came in to refresh Murray's morphine patch.

'It won't be a patch on the last one,' he quipped. I made my goodbyes and headed back out onto the ward.

I had one more person I was meant to visit. However, as I stepped out of Murray's room, Amanda came over to tell me that this one wasn't feeling very well. That she'd had to call it off.

'It's a shame you couldn't do it another time,' she

explained. 'She was really looking forward to it.'

It left me wondering what to do next.

It seemed like making an effort to meet this woman was important. Amanda said that if I was able to try tomorrow, there'd be a good chance of her feeling a bit better. This seemed doable, so I decided I would spend the night in Leeds, then try to meet her in the morning before I went home. But when I looked online, there wasn't really anywhere nearby that I could stay.

'You could always stay here,' Amanda suggested.

I told her this was very kind, but I couldn't possibly justify taking up a bed in a hospice.

'No, we have a room for family members,' she told me. 'We offer it out to them if it's difficult for them to get home.'

I thanked her again, but it sounded like this bed was for something more important.

'No, it's fine,' she said. 'No one needs it today. It would just be sitting there.'

And so it came to pass that I slept that night on a fold-out sofa bed in a room at the back of the hospice. It took a little getting used to. I could still hear the sounds of the machines on the ward. I couldn't shake the feeling that I was somehow breaking the rules. But everyone had told me it was fine. And the room itself even came with an en-suite. I'd give them a solid five stars for service.

In the morning, I went to the cafeteria and had scrambled eggs on toast. Then I met up with Amanda, who took me off to my third and final door.

I waited outside the room as usual, before she came back

out to give me the all-clear.

When I walked in, a woman was sitting in an armchair with long, straight grey hair and bright blue eyes. She was wearing a blue dressing gown and had a respirator over her face.

'When I told Sharon what you were doing, her eyes lit up,' Amanda said. 'Now, take your time, OK?'

She stepped out of the room and left us to it.

There was a moment's silence. The space was filled with the hissing of the oxygen tank. When she finally spoke, Sharon did it between huge gasps of air.

I found out during our conversation that Sharon had a matter of days to live, that she'd already lived much longer than the doctors had predicted she would. She never told me what her illness was. I never asked. I just asked her what was important to her.

'Family,' she said, between gasps. 'When I die, I want all of the family to stay close. We've not always been in the past, y'know.'

I asked her if she'd been thinking about this more often than usual.

'Yes,' she said, her eyes welling up. 'Because you think you've got all the time in the world. And then you realise you don't.'

I watched as tears began to roll from her eyes and down her cheeks. They hit the edge of her oxygen mask, and were funnelled along the line between her skin and the plastic.

'My twin sister Jeanie is marvellous,' Sharon said. 'She comes every day. She'll sit and have her tea with me, wash me. Sometimes she doesn't get home till eight at night.'

I told Sharon that I'd been missing my own family recently. That I hadn't seen them as often as I'd have liked. That I wanted to take a break soon, to go and spend a bit more time with them.

'You need to go,' she said, through deep sobs. She pulled her mask off, speaking very clearly and slowly over the loud hissing of the oxygen. 'Take it from me,' she said. 'Don't leave it too late, Rowan. Go and see your family. Do it now.'

I made my goodbyes and headed for the door.

I went back to deliver Sharon's poem on Friday the 13th. Before I left the house, I turned on the TV and learned that Boris Johnson had become the next prime minster. Then I stepped out of the door and headed for the train to Leeds.

I knew where everyone's rooms in the hospice were now. There was no need for a guide. When I arrived, the receptionist gave me a pass and I headed up to Lewis' room, and then Murray's, who both thanked me heartily for what I'd written. Then I went to see Sharon.

I had no idea if she would still be here. It had been a few days, and she was already in quite a critical state. When I got to the right ward, I asked a passing nurse if I could go in. She told me Sharon wasn't feeling very well, that she'd have to go in and check.

The nurse came back out a moment later. She said it was OK, so long as I didn't stay too long.

When I went into her room Sharon was sitting in her armchair, slipping in and out of consciousness. I said hello and reminded her why I'd come. Then I read out her poem. When I'd finished, she said something very softly. But she was so weak, I couldn't make out what it was.

'Thank you,' she whispered, before nodding forward on to her legs.

I took her gently by the shoulders and pulled her upwards so she was propped against the armchair. I placed the poem on the table next to her, then stepped quietly out of the room, back into the rush and commotion of the world outside.

And When I Got the News
I Thought of You

And when I got the news I thought of you,
my only reason was to hold you close.
Those past mistakes, the plans I'd muddled through
were dull distractions from what mattered most.

Outside, the leaves were falling on the ground,
the children laughed as they walked home from school,
the sun was bright, the world was spinning round,
and suddenly it all slid into view.

Our lives are tightrope walks, so close to ruin,
the slightest breeze can knock us as we go,
yet rarely do we stop to take the view in,
so full of fear and fixed on what's below.

But now that fear has faded like a dream,
to hold you here is all there's ever been.

13

CHRISTMAS IN HEBBURN

A VERY ATHLETIC FRIEND OF MINE once gave me a piece of advice.

'Do you want to know the secret of jogging?' he said. 'First, go slow. Then, go slower. Then, go even slower than that.'

It turns out, I'm a natural at jogging.

The more I've carried this advice around with me, the more I've realised that it actually applies to lots of other things. They say Rome wasn't built in a day. And really, if anything is worth doing, it's probably going to take quite a long time to finish it. The secret to success, by my reckoning, is not the sweaty, desperate sprint. It is the slow, relentlessly persistent plod.

That said, if you're reading this and you are an Olympic sprinter, please ignore all of that. The secret to success for you is definitely the sprinting. The sweaty, desperate sprinting.

The advice of this friend had come back to me during my trip home from Leeds. I needed a minute to catch my breath.

I'd been hoping to learn about lots of different people on

this adventure. But when it came to St Gemma's, it felt like someone had shown me my own reflection instead. When Sharon told me to visit my family, it had hit me quite hard. I knew I owed it to her to do what she'd recommended.

I was beginning to understand why I'd been feeling a bit lonely recently. I was starting to see that, no matter how interesting and moving the conversations I was having with people on this journey were, there was a difference between spending time with strangers and spending time with those you hold close.

It seems glaringly obvious to say that now, but I was learning that it's not enough simply to take every interaction you have with a friend or family member and replace it by a conversation with a stranger.

You occupy quite an unusual space as a Door-to-Door Poet. People let you into their homes, they let their guards down, they sometimes share the most intimate and personal details of their lives with you. And in the times when this happened, it felt humbling and amazing and inspiring.

But, in a weird sort of way, I could see now that what I was doing was providing a kind of service. In the same way that you can have a fantastic conversation with a shopkeeper or a hairdresser, but you might not necessarily invite them to your birthday party, I was beginning to realise that my role as a Door-to-Door Poet was not really about making friends. And this had left me feeling a little bit lost.

One day I was doing an interview with a journalist from a local culture magazine.

'I just have one last question for you,' she said to me, as

we sat on a park bench next to a canal. 'What's important to you?'

It was meant to be a fun question. She wanted me to enjoy the opening lines that I'd used to start so many conversations so far. The trouble was, I couldn't think of an answer. I completely froze up.

I'd been so fixated on seeing this mission through to the end. The only important thing to me at the time seemed to be asking other people what was important to them. I'd forgotten what any of my own hobbies or opinions were. I'd forgotten who I was. I managed to laugh my way out of it, but on the way home I felt a bit hollow. I'd become, it seemed, some kind of recording device, with no real thoughts or feelings of my own.

On December the 20th, I decided to do something about this. I put an auto-reply on my emails. Rose and I put our thickest coats on and we took the extensive five-mile trek to my home town via the Metro train.

Christmas in Hebburn is a magical experience, sure to chase the sadness from even the coldest and deadest of hearts. Every year, the council wheels out a wooden shed with a Perspex screen in it. Within this shed is a life-sized plastic nativity scene, complete with polyethylene Jesus, Mary, Joseph, three wise men, plus an assortment of farm-yard animals.

This nativity scene is now so old that it predates all living memory. Like Stonehenge, or the pyramids, nobody quite knows how it was made, or what its exact function was intended to be. All we know is that, wherever it came from, it is an unwritten and sacred law that Christmas cannot be celebrated in Hebburn until the Perspex shed is placed in its rightful position in the town square.

We went past it on the way to my parent's house that year. The plastic models are so ancient that all the paint has faded from their bodies. The figures are just vaguely humanoid blobs of white – how I imagine all the celebrities would look if there was a heatwave in Madame Tussaud's. Still, when I looked up at those festive white blobs, I knew that somewhere, hidden in their plastic folds, was a smile. And I knew that the season of merriment and joy was truly upon us.

I feel like I've been a bit mean about Hebburn so far. The truth is that, these days, Hebburn is a very different place to the one I grew up in. We have an Asda. And a Domino's. The council has long since got rid of the broken fountain. All around town, on the sites of demolished tower blocks, new-build estates are springing up, with billboards offering exciting deals for the first-time buyer. The fear that some-one might one day open a deli or, worse, a micro-brewery, has become a very real and ever-present threat. And though Hebburn still valiantly resists much of what you'd describe as gentrification, there's no denying that the place is changing.

I brought a keg of ale to my parent's house. We had a long-overdue family catch-up. It was dead nice. After a few days, Rose went over to Lincolnshire and I stayed on to celebrate the festive season at home.

It was during this time that something quite wonderful happened. Something kind of magical. Because I came, very briefly, into the possession of a drone.

My grandad dropped it off for me on Christmas day. It wasn't a present. At least, not in the traditional sense of the word.

He told me that someone had stolen his credit card details and had started ordering loads of stuff online. For reasons that never became clear, the thief hadn't changed the delivery address, so all of that stuff had begun to arrive at my grandad's house. The credit card company refunded him the money and he was allowed to keep the items too, which was pretty jammy really.

I've often wondered if my grandad was actually behind this all along. He is sadly now no longer with us, so there's no way of finding out for sure. He was always a very honest kind of guy, but he did go a bit crazy when it came to internet shopping. Just before he died, he went through a phase of ordering hundreds of identical belts – belts he could never possibly have had any use for.

I'm not sure if he'd accidentally ordered the drone, or done it on purpose. If it was the latter, he may have figured out quite a bulletproof method for getting away with a spot of online fraud. Either way, he told me he had no use for the drone, so he came over and bequeathed it to me.

I must have been talking quite excitedly about this for the rest of the day. That would be the best explanation for why, the following morning, I was awoken from my post-ale stupor by a knock at the door. It was my cousin, Ryan.

'Are we going to fly this drone then or what?'

He agreed to wait until I'd at least had a cup of tea, then

we walked over to the nearest park.

Ryan is the same age as me and probably just about as childish. One of my favourite memories is of him, aged nine, mixing together all the soft drinks in his kitchen to try and invent new ones. 'Toffe': tea and coffee. 'Jea': juice and tea. You get the idea. Anyway, he's an engineer now and I like to think that, in some small way, those early culinary experiments really set him on that path.

We got to the park and I lifted the drone out of the box. It was all sleek and black with orange propellors. It looked quite complicated. The instructions were in Chinese and there was no English version anywhere to be found.

We put the drone in the middle of a football field, then took a few steps back and turned on the remote. It burst into life, whirring like a hairdryer, hovering a few metres above the ground.

So far so good. But then I pushed the button to make it go higher. And that's when it all started to go a bit pear-shaped.

The drone was rising – that wasn't the problem. The problem was that there didn't seem to be a way to make it stop. I pressed the down button, but this had no effect. I pressed it again. I held it down. Nothing. The drone just went higher and higher.

It was gathering quite a speed now. Up it soared, up and up and up, like a lost balloon, till it was nothing but a flashing speck in the clouds. And then we watched this tiny black grain as it fell from the atmosphere and hurtled towards a distant tree. I laughed till it hurt.

Standing under that tree a few moments later, we went

about trying to dislodge the drone, which was now stuck in one of the highest branches. It was about thirty metres up – far too high to reach, or even climb, especially with said hangover. We resorted to throwing sticks and stones instead.

A man on a mobility scooter and his ten-year-old grandson walked past. The child asked what we were doing

'Our drone is stuck in that tree,' we told him.

'Oh no.'

He immediately started to help us, throwing more rocks and sticks to try and dislodge it.

Soon after, a woman came walking past with her dog.

'What's wrong?' she asked.

'There's a drone stuck in the tree,' the boy said.

She passed us one of those special ice-cream scoop devices for throwing tennis balls to dogs. I think she thought it was the little boy's drone. I was about to correct her, but that ball looked like it'd really do the trick, and I wasn't sure if she'd give it to us without the small-boy as a pity factor.

We established pretty early on that Ryan was the best shot. The rest of us stood there watching, or collecting the ball, as he took turns throwing it, sometimes wildly missing, sometimes getting close enough to bring about a stifled murmur of anticipation.

A small crowd had begun to gather.

'What's going on?'

'Those boys have got their drone stuck in that tree.'

'What's a drone?'

'It's a bit like a helicopter.'

'Like a toy helicopter?'

'Sort of, just with more propellors.'

'They're quite expensive you know.'

'I know, my grandson has one.'

'The day after Christmas as well.'

'What a shame.'

I didn't have the heart to tell all these people that the drone was potentially stolen goods. Or that I'd never had any interest in owning or flying one until yesterday. Anyway, I didn't care. It was mine now and I wanted it back.

But as the winter sun began to set, we collectively accepted defeat and decided to call it a day. The crowd dispersed and we went our separate ways, each back to our own lives and concerns. I went to my parent's house and tried to cheer myself up with a block of Wensleydale and some crackers.

And then something quite lovely happened. Because the next day, someone had found the drone lying at the bottom of the tree. They had put a picture of it on social media. By a few degrees of separation, a friend of a friend of that person knew Ryan. Ryan came over to my parents' house the day after, drone in hand. It was a bit muddy and scuffed, but otherwise completely fine.

Imagine, for a minute, how many people stopped to try and solve that problem. Imagine how many opportunities they had to do something unhelpful, or even cruel, for their own personal gain. And I know it might seem silly, but this encounter reminded me what this whole adventure was really about. It was about the small, everyday connections we can make. It was about the fact that, really, people can be so helpful and kind for no reason at all, other than the fact that they want to and it seems like the right thing to do.

And no, you cannot replace your loved ones with strangers. You can't spend all of your time away from the people you care about and hope to not feel lonely. But in the same way that we need the people closest to us, I could see now that we needed these random interactions just as much. Because if we spend all of our time avoiding strangers, it's very easy to feel like they only ever wish to cause us harm.

Yet, so often on this journey, I was discovering just how much this wasn't the case.

I left my parents' house with a new-found sense of purpose. I'd remembered the point of what I was doing. What's more, I'd remembered who I really was in the process: I was the man who got drunk and flew his drone into a tree.

Christmas in Hebburn

Christmas in Hebburn isn't cinematic,
it isn't chestnuts on an open fire.
The bits that spring to mind are less dramatic,
they are not soundtracked by a festive choir.

It's Mam besieged with Sellotape and gifts
at quarter past eleven Christmas Eve,
as Dad steps in unsteady from The Longship,
a heavy afternoon out on the peeve.

It's getting to my nana's bungalow
and squeezing in a corner of the kitchen,
the living room filled up and fit to blow
with hordes of overstimulated children.

It's rushing to-and-fro from house to house
to make it back in time to eat the roast,
a frantic whistle-stop around the town
to chuck some gifts about then hit the road.

But outside, there's a stillness in the streets,
as if life's complications are on pause.
The calmness that descends when shots have ceased,
the closing of some long-forgotten war.

And though you know that it can't last forever,
everyone you pass seems more awake,
more open to the presence of each other,
even if it's only for a day.

14

FOLKESTONE

IT WAS NOW THE 5TH OF FEBRUARY 2020 and I was sitting in the passenger seat of a red Ford Fiesta, speeding down a motorway, somewhere along the coast of Kent.

'People don't realise how difficult life is for refugees,' Dan mused, as he flipped the indicators on. 'They think they're sorted now. They've got a nice house, someone to look after them. But it's not like that.'

To my left was a wide, flat field, extending out towards the sea. I could just about make out the white cliffs of Dover. As we approached the top of a hill, I looked down at a small town nestled in the valley below, a sprawl of semi-detached houses, the edge of a beach. It looked still and incredibly peaceful.

I'd arrived in Dover the day before, taking the walk from the train station into the centre of town. Along the way, I'd passed four-storey Georgian houses, a council estate, the outline of the town's castle, partially obscured by the local Esso garage.

I'd checked into the Castle House Guest House, a comfortable lodging that seemingly hadn't been decorated since

1972. I remember the owner wanted to make extra sure I didn't want any porridge for breakfast the next day. In fact, she'd seemed positively amazed that I didn't.

'And you're absolutely sure you don't want some porridge?' she said, for the third time, as if a humble fried breakfast with all of the trimmings could never be enough to sustain any grown adult for more than a few minutes.

In the morning, sans porridge, I took the walk across town to the offices of an organisation called Migrant Help. I pushed open the double doors, headed up the laminate stairs and told the receptionist what I was there for. I don't think she really believed me.

Migrant Help is an organisation that works with refugees and asylum seekers. They assist people with a lot of different things: arranging housing, finding English lessons or social support. Pretty much anything you could be struggling with when you arrive in a new and strange land, Migrant Help will try and do something about it.

I'd got in touch with them because I was interested in what life might be like for someone who had only just arrived in this country – someone who had no concept of a North/South divide. At least not for the time being, anyway.

The mood in the country had been changing too. On the 31st of January, Britain had officially left the EU. I was feeling a bit concerned about the way this might affect the lives of these people.

I'd spoken on the phone to a very helpful and enthusiastic woman called Jitka, who was the charity's Head of Communications. She'd handed me over to Dan, a case worker, who I was told was in touch with a number of Syrian families in a town called Folkestone. I explained what I'd been up to, what I was planning, and Dan said he'd be more than happy to bring me along on one of his regular visits.

Migrant Help had also offered to send an Arabic interpretor with us too. I'd never worked with an interpretor before. Suddenly, everything felt very official. I was now aware that there was a small team of people being employed to support me. Staff were depending on me to be at certain places at certain times. I could no longer sleep in late, or stop in the middle of the day for extended donut breaks.

I'd met the translator, Eklas, in the Migrant Help offices shortly after I arrived. She was waiting for me at Dan's desk.

Eklas informed me that she'd just had a minor eye operation, and so would need to wear sunglasses for the entire day. Dressed in a sharp black suit with bright pink sunshades, it gave her the look of some A-list celebrity who was trying to avoid the press. As if to exaggerate this, I was told that, in the world of local interpretors, Eklas was quite the big mover and shaker.

'They love me in Kent,' she beamed as we walked across the car park that morning, looking and sounding every bit like Angelina Jolie.

But life for Eklas had not exactly been a Hollywood fantasy. She told me later that she'd come here from Iraq in 1999, having taken a perilous journey in the back of a lorry.

'I nearly died lots of times,' she said, completely matter-of-fact, as if she was describing a broken toaster or a punctured tyre. She spoke about the way this influenced her work.

'When I'm interpreting, I'm often putting myself in the other person's shoes. I understand a lot of what these people are feeling.'

Today Eklas had the unenviable task of trying to translate some of my poetry. As we went over the plan in Dan's car, she'd seemed a little daunted by the prospect, reading and re-reading the printed sheet I'd passed her. I told her not to worry. Most people didn't understand what I was saying at the best of times, even if they spoke English fluently.

We were heading off to meet person number twenty-five. Or rather, people number twenty-five. Because today we were going to meet a series of families instead of individuals. This, like my visit to St Gemma's, and St Basil's before that, had been pre-arranged. And though a part of me was now craving the thrill of bothering people at random on their doorsteps, I could understand why it needed to be a bit more organised.

We'd left enough time for around an hour at each house. I was told this was a good idea. Syrian people, Eklas explained, were famed for their love of hospitality. It was nigh on impossible to engage in any kind of social visit without them laying out an elaborate feast first.

A shy person at heart, I can sometimes feel a little awkward when people go to a lot of trouble over me. But Dan and Eklas had assured me that there really was no way around this. It was simply the way it was done. And in the end I'd decided there were worse customs to be subjected to. After all, no one was making me do bingo, or karaoke.

We pulled into a quiet street later that day, five minutes from the Channel tunnel. We all got out of the car and headed over to a tall, red-brick terraced house with a small front garden. There was a mobility scooter in the front. I could see the outline of someone waving at us from behind a curtain.

Dan tapped the knocker and I followed him and Eklas inside. We took our shoes off and I shuffled through into the living room to be greeted by Leila and Saad.

Leila and Saad were a married couple in their forties. Leila was wearing a khaki green *khimar* and matching headscarf. She had deep brown eyes. Saad was sitting on a cushion on the floor in a white polo-neck jumper, his greying hair stylishly slicked back, making him look a bit like George Clooney.

The room was sparsely decorated. A mirror hung above a wooden mantle, a family picture resting on top of it. There was a small black sofa, an old armchair. They both greeted us warmly and invited us to sit down. I found a space next to Eklas.

After this, Leila began rushing backwards and forwards in a flurry from the kitchen, covering a small coffee table with sweets and nibbles: chocolates, crisps, baklava, a middle eastern sweet called halawa. She then came back with some traditional Arabic coffee in small cups and saucers. It was super-strong rocket fuel. Really tasty, and spiced with cardamom. Any attempts to politely decline these were humorously overpowered.

As she laid out the table, Saad showed us an app on his

phone that told him which way Mecca was. He joked, via Eklas, about the irony of his name. 'Saad' in Arabic, he told me, means happy. This, as you can imagine, had led to a number of hilarious misunderstandings.

Having got ourselves comfortable, and having already consumed more sugar than I'd really like to admit, it was time to get started. The first job was for me to explain why I'd come, to show Leila and Saad my introductory poem. Eklas pulled out her printed sheet and then looked across at me expectantly.

No one had ever translated one of my poems before. Truth be told, it made me wish I'd put a bit more effort into writing it. And there's nothing like watching someone recite what you've written to make you realise just what kind of a knock-on effect your own idleness can have.

'I'm a Door-to-Door Poet,' I began, before nervously glancing over at Eklas.

And off she went, dutifully translating every word, every clunky rhyme. We went through it, one line at a time, with me speaking, then Eklas, then me again. I didn't really know what to do when she was talking, so I just stared down at the carpet and listened. To be fair, it sounded much better in Arabic. I learned that 'Door-to-Door' is 'Albab 'iilaa Albab'.

'Maybe you dropped your smartphone and it fell down the toilet,' I said, and Saad and Leila both chuckled. Despite the language barrier, we seemed to have found some common ground.

I asked them both what was important to them. I made a point of mentioning that this could be absolutely anything

169

– something small and insignificant. Earlier that day, Eklas had had some questions about this herself.

'Is there any information you would like me to get out of them?' she'd said, explaining the nature of interpreting, the way you often have to read between the lines. I'd told her no, not really. There wasn't anything I wanted them to say or not say. As long as these people were talking about something that was important to them, that was all that really mattered.

But as the conversation unfolded, it became clear that Leila already had something on her mind. Something she very much wanted to get off her chest.

She reached into a drawer and pulled out a photo. On it was an image of two small children, aged five and seven. They were sitting on a pile of rubble, looking up at the camera, scared and confused. The smallest child had a red stain around his mouth which I believed to be blood.

'My life has been very hard,' Leila told me.

She explained that she and Saad were visiting her auntie when the bombs had started falling. When they got back and found their home completely destroyed, they had made the decision to flee the country. With no car and no public transport, they walked 130 kilometres from western Syria across the border into Iraq, carrying their children and the last of their possessions. When they arrived, they were housed in a refugee camp – a makeshift shack with a tarpaulin roof. This, at the time, was the best they could possibly hope for.

Leila told me it was during this period that she was diagnosed with cancer. It was very difficult to get the treatment she needed, and she had to walk a very long way to the hospital. By this point, Saad had lost the use of his legs, so he wasn't able to look after both children on his own. This meant that Leila did all of these journeys with her youngest child, sometimes staying away from home for more than twenty days at a time. Having received a course of chemo, she'd then take the long walk back to the refugee camp, feeling drained and nauseous from the treatment.

This is still one of the bravest and most incredible things I have ever heard anyone say.

'One day, I was alone with my son,' she told me. 'I was too weak to feed him. He was crying. I will never forget this.'

There were tears running down her face.

After four years, Leila and her family were offered the chance to move to the UK as part of a UN resettlement programme. They had flown over on the 12th of February the previous year.

'Two days before Valentine's Day,' Saad said, smiling.

They spoke about how things had changed since they'd arrived.

'We are much more relaxed now,' Leila told me. 'The people here are very kind.'

And though she had experienced hardship on a level I could never begin to understand, I also got the feeling that there was a fierce resilience here too. A pride in having taken on the most impossible challenge – and having actually won.

'Before this happened, I was very shy,' Leila explained. 'Now I am strong. I am a strong woman.'

It was a message that I was to hear echoed in the mouths of many people that day.

An hour later, I'd met Nour, an eighteen-year-old who had stayed in her home city of Damascus for three years after the bombing started, determined to finish her studies.

'When you've lived through a war, you feel like there's nothing you can't achieve,' she'd told me.

Then there was Shirin, whose son Ali had also become very sick after they fled Syria.

'My children are the most important thing,' she'd explained. 'I would do anything for them.'

I had started the day wanting to keep my questions as open-ended as possible. I was hoping that, by doing this, it might give the families I spoke to the chance to talk on any subject they liked. By the end of the day, I'd realised just how pointless this had really been.

I could see now that the war had affected every element of these people's lives. It was the ground zero from which everything else was measured. It informed every thought, every emotion, every decision and every conversation.

Hearing these stories, it had also never been clearer to me how important it was to offer a safe refuge to people like this. Although it was a welcome change for them, the move to the UK hadn't brought an end to their suffering. Like everyone I spoke to that day, Leila still had relatives living in Syria – something she told me was a constant source of worry and fear.

I went back to deliver the poems on the 26th of February, Dan driving once again, Eklas on translation. Leila and Saad greeted us at the door. For the second and final time, we sat down in their living room while I lost myself in a haze of caffeine and sugar.

Leila had given me a huge subject. Despite my best efforts, I'd had to shorten it. Before I read her poem, I felt like I needed to explain this. To mention that, if anything didn't seem right, I could change it.

She said this was fine.

'If you told the whole story it would have to be a film,' she added.

I read it out.

Leila explained that she used to write a lot of poetry herself. She was the top of her class for Arabic. She was a big fan of the famous Syrian love poet, Nizar Qabbani.

She told me that my name was actually Kurdish, that it's related to plants.

'"Rowan" is a word for when something grows very quickly and healthily in the ground,' she said.

We spoke about how, in English, Rowan is the name of a tree. We all wondered about the way this word might have travelled from her home to mine, a message migrating across centuries and cultures.

Then Leila said something to Eklas in Arabic. They started to giggle. Eklas took her empty coffee cup and flipped it over on to a saucer.

'I'm not even going to explain,' she said, before flipping it back.

She passed the cup to Leila, who proceeded to look at the stain in the bottom. After a minute, I realised she was reading her fortune.

'It's just for fun,' Eklas noted. 'She says she can see a picture of a girl – of my daughter. She's telling me she'll have a good future.'

We started to make our goodbyes. I told both Leila and Saad that I hoped it wouldn't be too long before we crossed paths again.

And then Saad mentioned the news. Because, as I'd been darting back and forth between Newcastle and Kent, something had been quietly bubbling away in the background. It had begun with a few minor stories. Something about a place called Wuhan. Pretty soon, schools in Germany had started closing. Soon after that, Italy was facing an epidemic. Last week, the UK had had its first confirmed cases. And the warnings about this new virus were beginning to feel pretty real.

Saad told us he was thinking about taking his kids out of school, just to be on the safe side.

As we waved goodbye to him and Leila, I was feeling like I might not have very long left to finish this adventure. That my days as a Door-to-Door Poet could be running out.

And if this was really how it was all going to end, I knew I needed to try something big, something stupid, something seemingly impossible…

Forwards

She tells me,
when the bombing started,
she was at her auntie's.
She remembers
coffee cups clashing,
falling to the floor,
holding her breath
in silent prayer.

At home,
she took a photo of her
sons on the rubble;
she needed something palpable now
words were powerless,
decisions left unspoken.

It's 130 kilometres to Iraq.
In the midday sun,
with a child on your back,
it's measured in sweat,
painful breaths.

At the end of the road
there's a tarpaulin shack
where the storms break in,
where the sickness

squeezes your skull,
heavy as a desert boulder.

I ask what kept her going.
She tells me
the question is irrelevant.
When your days are swayed by
the unknown,
when the route home is long closed,
it's no longer about stopping or starting.
Forward is the only option.

15

FENHAM

I LEARNED A LOT DURING MY VISIT to the Syrian families of Folkestone. And really, I walked away from most places feeling like I'd gained an important new perspective. It was interesting to find out about so many peoples' hopes and concerns. It turns out talking to lots of strangers can do wonders for your general knowledge.

A year before I visited Folkestone, I tested Door-to-Door Poetry out in a place called Fenham, which is a neighbourhood in the west end of Newcastle. There's a big mix of different cultures. There's quite a large Asian community.

I went knocking on a street called Wingrove Gardens. I met a load of friendly and enthusiastic residents here. All of them were more than happy to get involved. This included a man called Corey, who asked for one about his local barbershop, Salman, who asked for one about what music would sound like in the future. And Sami.

Sami answered the door in a white topi and a grey jumper. He was holding his granddaughter at the time, a two-year-old girl with pigtails, who smiled and waved throughout the whole conversation.

When I asked Sami what was important to him, he replied instantly.

'God,' he told me. 'God is everything.'

Sami went on to explain that he was a Muslim, that this was something which helped him to live his life in a way that he felt was good and right.

I told Sami I would love to write him a poem about Islam. The only problem was, I didn't know very much about it.

'There's a mosque across the road,' he said, pointing behind me. 'You could find out about it there.'

This came as a bit of a surprise. I hadn't actually noticed there was a mosque on this street. In fact, so taken aback was I that there really was an actual mosque here, I even turned around to check. As if Sami might have made some kind of a mistake. As if he might have just got a bit confused about where his local temple was, despite it being, quite literally, across the road from his house.

How I'd managed to miss this major landmark on such a small residential street is still beyond me. But sure enough, when I turned around that day, there it was. The Wingrove Mosque.

I felt a bit funny about showing up at the mosque unannounced. I didn't want to interrupt anyone in the middle of something important. It felt like it would be more polite to call ahead first. So I got in touch with a poet called Wajid, who happens to be a Muslim and who also lives in the area. He passed me the number for the mosque's imam. An imam, I learned, was a bit like a priest or a vicar in a Christian church. I called up Imam Kola later that day and he told me

I'd be very welcome to come along and have a look around.

I'd never visited a mosque before. On the bus there, I found myself very seriously questioning my choice of dress. It dawned on me that I was wearing black skinny jeans and a t-shirt with The Clash written on it. Along the bottom of this was the title of the song, 'Straight To Hell'.

Was this really suitable attire for a trip to a mosque? Maybe I should have worn something a bit more formal. Smart casual? What was the correct dress code for this occasion, anyway?

Whatever it was, I was now pretty sure that this wasn't it. But it was too late to go back. I was just going to have to get on with it. The plan was to head in there and try to get out as quickly as I could, while breaking as few religious taboos as possible.

So, at 18:38, on a cold and wet Wednesday evening, dressed in what was quite possibly the most inappropriate t-shirt anyone had ever worn for such a purpose, I arrived at the Wingrove Mosque.

I stood at the entrance and took a minute to catch my breath. The building was covered in shiny red tiles. There were green minarets at each corner. Above me, I could just about make out a dome on the roof, a small gold crescent.

I headed up a ramp to a bright green door. I was greeted by a young man, who I think could tell that I didn't exactly know my way around. He invited me to take my shoes and socks off and pointed to a white shelf with a number of trainers and sandals stacked on them.

This was the moment I learned why you should never

wear Doc Marten boots during a visit to a mosque. After many minutes of unlacing, I stepped into the hallway and was greeted by Imam Kola.

Imam Kola was a jolly-looking man in his fifties. He was dressed in a cream *thobe,* and had an epically distinguished beard. He shook my hand and led me into a little office with a small wooden desk in it. He offered me a dried date. I accepted.

Imam Kola told me he'd been intrigued to hear about my adventures. He said that, actually, there was a big link between poetry and Islam.

'Before Muhammad wrote the Qur'an, the site of the Kaaba in Mecca was used for poetry competitions,' he explained.

He told me that every tribe in the local area would have their own poet. These poets were responsible for recording the stories of their communities. In an age before the news or social media, this job was pretty important. These people, as they say in the world of business, were wearing a lot of different hats. They were storytellers and they were rhymers. They were journalists, historians and philosophers. Most importantly, perhaps, they were also entertainers.

Imam Kola explained that, every year, these poets would gather at the site of Mecca and recite epic verses in praise of their tribe. Journeys they had made. Battles they had won. The event would last for hours. At the end, a winner would be declared and the victorious poem would be hung up in the Kaaba for the rest of the year, until the next competition, when the tribe poets would go head-to-head once again.

It struck me that this must surely be the seventh-century version of a rap battle.

'When Muhammad wrote the Qur'an,' Imam Kola explained, 'everyone agreed that it was not human. The Arabic was too pure. After that, the text was hung up permanently in the Kaaba, and all of the other poetry was taken down. They knew it could never be beaten.'

Meaning that, as far as I could gather, the Qur'an is the oldest recorded example of the mic drop.

Imam Kola took me on a tour of the building. He showed me the room where people wash before prayer, then he took me upstairs to see the main hall.

It was a large, empty space with white walls and a pink carpet. I noticed there were red lines running diagonally along it. Imam Kola told me these lines were there to show people where to sit.

I noticed this big clock at the front of the room. It was shiny and silver and had a lot of different faces on it. I learned that the different faces represented the different times of the day when you're supposed to pray. These times change throughout the year, based on the position of the sun and the moon.

'On a Friday this room will be completely full,' Imam Kola told me. 'It's a bit like Sunday in a Christian church. If you want to know what a mosque is all about, why don't you come back and see it for yourself?'

I decided to take him up on his offer.

Two days later, I went back to the Wingrove Mosque. I made sure to get there nice and early, but there were already hundreds of people filing upstairs when I arrived. I spotted Imam Kola in amongst the crowd, a queue of followers all waiting patiently to ask for his sage advice.

Everyone seemed really happy to see me. People were smiling and waving. A little boy ran over and shook my hand. It was very different to the Roman Catholic churches I got dragged to as a kid.

I followed the crowd upstairs, hoping I could find somewhere to sit that was discreet and out of the way. I was under no illusions that I had absolutely no clue what I was supposed to be doing at this ceremony.

I managed to find a space in the back corner. I sat down and watched as hundreds of the congregation began to filter in and take their places.

In the blink of an eye, the room was packed from wall-to-wall. There were men of all ages. I don't think you could have fitted another body in there if you tried. Not even a very small one.

Soon after this, the prayer started. Imam Kola recited verses from the unbeatable poem. People stood and kneeled in unison. They bowed their heads. It was fascinating.

To see this many people all moving as one was something in itself. But to be a part of it, to be shoulder-to-shoulder with them, was something else entirely. I tried my best to keep up with the pace. It felt a bit like not knowing the rules to musical chairs. Without warning, everyone would suddenly stand up, and I'd be left sitting there on my own. Then, just as I'd got comfortable, everyone would kneel again, and I'd be left standing, the sole upright person in a sea of curled backs.

I was just about getting the hang of it when everyone turned their head to the side. The ceremony, it seemed, was over. People began to slowly filter out of the room, calmly descending the stairs, walking back towards the front door.

I often think about this visit to the Wingrove Mosque. It was one of many unexpected side quests on my travels as a Door-to-Door Poet.

It was exciting that this chance encounter had led me down a rabbit hole. That it had become an opportunity to learn more.

And as my adventures ran their course, I'd often found myself feeling grateful for these moments. For what they were offering me.

On the surface, I was supposed to be getting ideas for poems. And I was definitely doing that. But it didn't take long for me to realise these visits were doing something much more important. They were giving me a different perspective. They were turning me into a more fully formed human being.

Wingrove Mosque

I

find space,

watch the white walls fill

to the brim with an ocean of people; 400 slow

and calm droplets from the

washroom. Water is

a precious

gift.

Imam

Kola sings in

quarter tones, standing atop

an oak throne, two branches either side a crisp

autumn leaf. The crowd all hum to

agree, the breath of

a sleeping

giant.

Then,

perfect silence, all

stand as one, bend at the waist,

rest on knees, touch the floor with foreheads.

A flat line across the ocean,

as still and peaceful as

a glass of

water.

16

BILLIONAIRES' BOULEVARD

It was Monday the 2nd of March 2020 and I was standing on a busy road, just outside Kensington Palace Gardens.

Cars and buses sped behind me. Pedestrians pushed past, completely uninterested in my endeavours.

In front of me was a white stone archway. Past that was a row of huge old elm trees. Between their branches, I could make out the front of a pink mansion.

London. I always knew I was going to take Door-to-Door Poetry here. Ever since that fateful conversation with the posh-sounding woman in Edinburgh. And it felt like, if I still wanted to try this, it was probably best to get on with it pretty soon.

It didn't take a genius to figure out that my days as a Door-to-Door Poet were numbered. I'd arrived in London just as the number of Covid cases had jumped from two to thirty-nine. The UK's chief medical officer was now saying that there was not much chance of stopping this. It was no longer a case of 'if', but a case of 'when'.

I took a walk around town to get my bearings. I passed through Westminster, stopping briefly at Buckingham

Palace, squeezing through crowds of tourists armed with fanny packs and selfie sticks.

On the face of it, everything in the Big Smoke looked tickety-boo.

But everywhere you went, there was a funny kind of atmosphere. People seemed more uncomfortable than usual. It felt like we were all collectively walking on a frozen pond, knowing that, at any minute, someone's foot was going to break through the surface, plunging us all into a cold and unfathomable chaos.

Whatever I did next, I knew this could be the end of Door-to-Door Poetry for some time. And I was feeling like I needed to go out with a bang. To finish with something so incredibly unlikely, so ridiculous, that the very thought of it was laughable.

With this in mind, there seemed no better place to visit than Kensington Palace Gardens.

Sometimes known as 'Billionaires' Boulevard', Kensington Palace Gardens has some of the most expensive properties in the country. It was home at the time to Chelsea FC owner Roman Abramovich, as well as Lakshmi Mittal, one of the richest men in the world.

As you can probably imagine, I didn't have the contact details for the richest man in the world. This meant that, unlike my last few visits, I was planning to knock on these doors at random. To go back to basics. And even though I'd been missing the thrill of bothering people on their door-steps, I didn't actually think this was going to work. Did I?

To be honest, after the year I'd had, I didn't really know

any more. At the start of this adventure, I would never have considered trying something like this. But there was a time, I recalled, not so long ago, when I didn't think I could get away with this in Grantchester. Or in Boston. There was a time when I didn't think it was possible in my home town.

If there was one thing I'd learned from this journey so far, it was that it was important to try. And whatever happened next, I was emboldened by the knowledge that I was now very near the finishing line. I'd written poems for twenty-seven people. I only had to find three more to reach my target of thirty.

How hard could it be?

Feeling ready for whatever lay on the other side, I took a deep breath and stepped through the archways onto Kensington Palace Gardens.

To my right was a little prefab building, flanked by a red and white automatic barrier. As I looked over at this, I was instantly confronted by a security guard.

'Hi there, my name is Rowan and I don't want any money or anything. I'm going all around the country writing poems for people, for free, on any subject they like. I wondered if you thought anyone on this street might be interested?'

The guard eyed me suspiciously.

'It's mostly diplomats who live here, sir.'

I told him this was fine. I asked him if he thought any of these diplomats might like a poem. He told me that they would not and asked me to leave immediately.

I turned around and walked back out of the archways.

OK. This wasn't exactly a surprise. I had a feeling that my

biggest problem today would be security. I was pretty sure there would be a lot of gates and guards around a place like this. That there would be intercoms.

An intercom was probably the worst thing I could hope for. It's quite difficult to explain Door-to-Door Poetry at the best of times, but even more so when it's through a tiny speaker from out in the street. I knew if I didn't get in front of some people face-to-face, there wasn't really much hope of this working.

That said, I didn't think I'd be able to meet anyone face-to-face in Grantchester, and I'd found a way to make it work there. Maybe I could find a way here, too?

I walked down Bayswater Road until I got to Palace Gardens Terrace. It was a row of four-storey houses, all with barrel-arched doorways and stone balustrades above the windows. Every house was painted a blindingly brilliant white.

If I couldn't get to Billionaires' Boulevard, Palace Gardens Terrace seemed like the next best choice. It was the neigh-bouring street, it still looked fancy. Crucially for me, there were no intercoms and not a security guard in sight.

I walked up to the first house, up a set of wide, spotless black steps, to a shiny black door with a golden letterbox. The yard was decorated with black and white tiles like a chessboard. I tapped on the knocker. It made a deep, hollow rattle every time I let it go.

A man came out in a baseball cap and a red anorak. I explained myself. I showed him my introductory poem.

'Sorry, I'm not in a position to discuss something like this,' he said, as if I had just offered him a timeshare in a luxury condo. I asked him if he might be in a position to discuss it at a later date. He told me he wasn't sure, so I left him to it.

I carried on along the street.

Knocking on doors here was quite disorientating. Every property looked exactly the same. Not just similar, but absolutely identical. It created the sensation of *Groundhog Day* – as if I was knocking on the same door over and over again and getting variations on the same reply. If I'd taken some footage of the answers I got, you would be forgiven for thinking that's exactly what happened.

The replies were various shades of no. The people who came out often sounded American, apart from one woman who was clearly from Yorkshire. At one door, a lady in a fur coat appeared before I'd even knocked. She seemed quite annoyed by my presence. I left quickly and managed to jam my finger in the metal gate as I went. A few seconds later, my finger started bleeding. It was not a good look.

Outside another door, a man in a brown mac was on his way into the house.

'What are you?' he asked.

'I'm a Door-to-Door Poet,' I started. But I didn't get far.

'No!' he exclaimed, before swiftly walking inside.

A minute later, I overheard him talking to someone.

'There's a Door-to-Door Poet out there for Christ's sake!'

A little further along from this, I rang a bell and was unexpectedly buzzed in. The house smelled like an antiques shop. It was in the middle of being redecorated, the rooms above filled with the sounds of hammering and drilling. I

189

cautiously trod along the hallway, over a red carpet covered in plastic sheeting. I got to a mahogany door and knocked. A Russian lady in her thirties answered. She told me she thought I was the gas man.

I explained that I wasn't the gas man but I wondered if she might have a minute to spare. She said thanks, but no thanks.

I carried on along the street. It was more of the same. In fact, I was all but ready to give up on Palace Gardens Terrace when I spotted a woman heading through her gate on the way inside. She was wearing a blue parka and sunshades. She had very long, very shiny hair.

'I'm sure you must be really busy,' I said. 'But I was wondering if you had a minute?'

She said yes. I showed her my poem.

She told me her name was Mahika.

'I don't really like poetry,' she admitted, once I'd finished. 'But something I could read to my children would be nice.'

I asked what kinds of subjects her children were interested in.

'It should be about living in London,' she explained, instructively.

From the off, it was clear that Mahika had really taken the lead in this partnership. She seemed happy to direct the subject of the poem and tell me exactly what she wanted out of it. And I liked that about her. She didn't mess around.

I told her a poem about living in London sounded like a great idea. Only, I'd never lived in London before, so she might have to help me out a bit.

'It should be about the different things you can do here,' she advised. 'You can get a red bus tour around the neighbourhood, you can go on the London Eye. You can hear Big Ben from your window.'

'You can hear Big Ben from your window?!' I asked, amazed.

'No,' she confessed. 'This is just the kind of thing that you *might* experience if you lived in London.'

It was fair enough. Mahika was inviting me to use my imagination. What self-respecting poet could argue with that? Also, I was quite relieved that Big Ben wasn't actually that loud. For a minute, I wasn't sure how anyone would ever get to sleep around here.

We started to talk about what London meant to her.

'Everyone is welcome. That's what London means to me.'

I mentioned the stereotype of Londoners being a little anti-social.

'I think the only people who believe in those stereotypes are people who haven't lived here. We're a bigger city, and that will always affect things. But...actually,' she said, glancing at her phone, 'I really have to go now. Do you have everything you need?'

I ran over the plan for the delivery and made my goodbyes. She waved and headed back inside.

It was a brief encounter. But it didn't make it any less exciting. I had persuaded an actual resident of London to let me write a poem for them. And I only had two more people to go before I'd reached my target of thirty.

Admitting this to myself felt a little surreal. Granted, it was proving a bit more difficult in Kensington than I'd hoped. But there was no denying that the end was now tantalisingly close. There were butterflies in my stomach. My hands had begun to shake.

I tried the rest of the houses on Palace Gardens Terrace, but I had no luck. I began to wonder if a change of scenery might make it a little easier. I walked to the nearest station and took the tube to Belgravia.

Belgravia is another district with an eye-watering abundance of wealth. I stepped out of the station at Hyde Park Corner and was plunged into the insane traffic of the Wellington Arch. I walked along Grosvenor Crescent, spotting the embassies of various countries along the way: Belgium, Argentina, Romania, Bolivia, the United Arab Emirates. Bouncers in black suits with sunshades flanked every door. Occasionally, a delegate would step out dressed in a Louis Vuitton suit.

I wondered why all the embassies had ended up here. Did they arrange it in advance? Or did it just kind of snowball? Did the staff at the different embassies ever meet up for a drink after work? At Christmas, maybe? If not, this was a seriously missed opportunity. Imagine it. You could do a pub crawl from embassy to embassy. In one night, you could get completely plastered under the jurisdiction of every major government in the world. If you're reading this, and you happen to work in one of these embassies, think about it. People would pay good money for something like that.

A few minutes later, I got to a long street that overlooked a narrow park. This is the spot I'd been searching for. A place that fitted the bill of being a challenge but without, I hoped, being too heavily guarded in the process. That place was Eaton Square.

Eaton Square is another row of massive terraces. Built out of sandstone, each door is framed by these huge stone porticos, held up with Roman columns.

I'd picked it mostly because of the list of previous residents. Eaton Square has been home over the years to the likes of bearded spy-man Sean Connery, as well as Neville 'I've-got-a-magic-ticket' Chamberlain. And it was a shame Neville Chamberlain was no longer with us, I thought to myself. If anyone could appreciate someone waving a meaningless bit of paper around on their doorstep, it would surely have to be him.

Unfortunately for me, as I got nearer the building, I could see that outside every door was a set of identical solid-gold intercoms. As I walked up the steps to the first house, I noticed that the properties were actually divided into flats, each with their own separate intercom, labelled with a letter from A to M. It was not good news.

I started to ring buzzer after buzzer, waiting for ten minutes outside every door. Every now and again, someone answered and politely declined.

'That sounds lovely,' an elegant voice replied. 'But I'm just in the middle of a yoga class.'

A little while after, a man in John Lennon spectacles passed me on his way inside.

'Don't ring any of the bells at this door,' he told me.

I missed them out and carried on.

I rang buzzer after buzzer, steadily working my way along the street, becoming less sure about my success with every press of the button. It was approaching the end of the day now. The sun was setting. I looked at my watch and realised I'd been knocking on doors for nearly six hours.

At one point, I stopped to take a picture and noticed that a very tall, very muscular-looking man in a bowler hat was walking towards me. I could see that he had an earpiece in, the curly wire disappearing into the collar of his shirt.

'Excuse me, sir,' he said, in the most threatening way anyone has ever said those words. 'Obviously, we've seen you going up and down the street here. I was just wondering what this is all about?'

I gave him the story.

'I see,' he replied, looking increasingly confused. 'Have you got a social media account we could use to keep an eye on you?'

I found the phrase 'keep an eye on you' quite unsettling.

Exactly how long would this man be keeping an eye on me for? For the rest of the day? For the rest of my life?

I passed him my card. He glanced at it silently.

'You're not planning on ringing all of the bells on this street, are you, sir?' he asked, as if the concept was only now beginning to fully sink in.

I told him I most definitely was.

'It's just, the bells here aren't really for ringing,' he told me.

I asked him what the bells, in that case, were for.

'Well, they are for ringing, obviously. But they're only for invited guests, I'm afraid. I'm going to have to ask you to move on.'

It was now dark and it was starting to rain. Mostly to spite the bowler-hatted man, I made a point of crossing the road and trying a few more houses, even though he'd told me not to. But the responses here were more of the same. And I could see, from the corner of my eye, the man in the bowler hat was always lurking, watching my every move from the shadow of the porticos.

I felt cold and intensely unwelcome. For the first time since I'd started, I gave up and left.

I walked back towards the tube station. I passed down Sedding Street and stopped to take a picture of an extravagantly decorated hairdresser's.

As I looked behind me, I swear, in the middle distance, I could see a bowler hat in the crowd. It was far away, but it was unmistakeable.

I turned around lots of times after that. I couldn't shake the feeling that I was being followed.

The Bowler-hatted Guard

There are matters on this earth
beyond explanation,
but the strangest one I ever passed
as I travelled far and near,
was on a very fancy street,
keeping calm and silent witness:
A bowler-hatted man
with a wire in his ear.

He was a security guard in a bowler hat,
a security guard in a bowler hat,
he was standing at the entrance
to a nice block of flats,
he was sorting the wheat
from society's chaff.

I've seen truffle on pizza,
I've seen dogs in prams,
I've seen priests in casinos,
I've seen cocktails in cans,
but I've never seen a bigger mix
of humble and high-class
than a security guard
in a bowler hat.

O what was the purpose?
What was achieved?
When they hired him as He-Man
but styled him as Jeeves?
Did the business believe
it was somehow more probable?
Were they making the cleaners
wear top hats and monocles?

Bowler-hatted guard,
would you ever confess
this uniform's bordering
on fancy dress?
Are you craving a black
baseball cap for your dome
now you look like the sidekick
of old Sherlock Holmes?

At the end of the day,
do you jump on a bus
to a home in a suburb
that's not quite so plush?
Do you fold up your trousers
and put on some jeans,
do you turn on the toaster
and heat up some beans?

Does your bowler hat live
in a box on the shelf?
Do you keep it a secret?
Do you value your health?
As you head to a pub
where the paint's wearing thin
and the owners don't care
who goes out or comes in.

Bowler-hatted man
do you feel out of place?
Do they wince at the sound of you
dropping an 'h'?
On the edge of a world
that is highly protected,
where you wear the same clothes
but you're never accepted.

17

LONDON LAYOVER

I HAD NO WAY OF TELLING WHY it had been so difficult on Eaton Square, or on Palace Gardens Terrace. Maybe it was because of the security. Maybe the people on these streets were just less comfortable talking to strangers. Then again, with everything else that was going on, it was difficult to say for sure.

The situation with Covid was getting more complicated by the minute. The number of cases had jumped to fifty-one. The government had switched from talking about 'herd immunity' and telling us there was nothing to worry about, to proposing lockdowns and limited social contact in the not-too-distant future.

It was hard to ignore the effect this was having on the project. Now when I went out knocking it felt like I was asking people to put even more trust in me than ever before. They had to trust that I was who I said I was. But they also had to trust I wasn't carrying some mysterious and menacing sickness too. That they weren't going to put their health at risk by talking to me.

I'd even begun to feel a bit weird about telling people I'd

been travelling around the country. I'd taken to saying I was going around 'the area' instead, as if that might somehow make it seem less dangerous.

Maybe this was the reason it hadn't worked in London. I suppose I'll never really know. All I knew was that I still needed to find two people to reach my target of thirty. And I didn't have very long left to do it.

The day after my visit to Eaton Square, I woke up and opened my laptop. I knew there wasn't going to be time to go back to Newcastle. If I wanted to find the two people I needed, I was going to have to keep moving.

The first thing I did was book myself a train ticket to my next location. But the journey wasn't until late that afternoon, and I still had Mahika's poem to write. So I decided to do some sightseeing first.

Mahika had asked for a poem she could read to her kids, a poem about the different things you could do if you lived in London. This seemed like a good opportunity to try some of these things out for myself. Purely for research purposes, of course. Not because they might be in any way fun or entertaining.

There hadn't been much time to ask Mahika what her children were interested in. To play it safe, I decided I'd take a visit to the Natural History Museum.

My thinking was that there's dinosaurs in there, and kids unanimously love dinosaurs, don't they? Also, I'd never actually been to the Natural History Museum and, with the collapse of civilisation now seeming like a very real and imminent threat, it felt like a good moment to tick this off the bucket list.

On the walk out of South Kensington station, I stopped to buy a cheese sandwich in one of the shops in the Underground. Possibly because I was wearing a grey overcoat, a man outside asked me if I was a lawyer, before going on to recite some of his poetry. He told me he had moved here from France, and from North Africa before that. He said he couldn't travel around very much these days, but he still loved to get out in the local countryside whenever he could.

The fact that someone had stopped me to recite a poem, instead of the reverse, felt special. I told the man a little about what I'd been up to. It seemed like, if anyone in this city could understand, it would be him. He wished me all the best with it and I made my goodbyes before continuing on my way.

Outside the Natural History Museum, the first thing I noticed was how much it looks like a church. I trust that Londoners and nerds will be able to forgive this brief foray into metaphor but, from the off, it seemed to me a veritable cathedral of science, with its pterodactyl gargoyles carved into the stonework.

After queueing for what seemed like a surprisingly short time, I stepped into the main hall and was confronted by a huge blue whale skeleton that was dangling from the ceiling.

It was really, really big. I don't think I'd ever taken the time to consider how big a blue whale actually is. But when you get up close to the bones of one, you can't help but feel impressed.

I knew enough about this place to know that there was supposed to be a diplodocus here. I found out that 'Dippy', as he's affectionately called, was currently on tour.

I considered the idea of going on tour with a dinosaur. I wondered how big his entourage was, what life on the road with Dippy would be like. I bet he's an absolute party animal. A tour with Dippy is no doubt one of rockstar proportions, night after night of chewing on ferns and sniffing cocaine, television sets thrown out of hotel rooms with reckless abandon.

Classes of children passed by in yellow hi-vis jackets, listening to their teachers, trying not to get distracted by the giant whale above them. I found the skull of the last lion to have ever lived in England. Later, I stopped to take a photo of a dissected giant sequoia trunk.

It was laid on its side against a wall. I looked at the hundreds of concentric circles running inside it, marking out each year of its long and eventful life.

This tree was 1,300 years old when it was chopped down. It was 101 metres tall. Next to the trunk, the museum had left some information, showing you what age the tree would have been at various moments in history, as well as what human beings were up to at that particular time.

In 537 AD, for example, this tree was a sapling. In 622 AD, the human population stood at 206 million, less than the current number of Americans. In 725 AD, the Buddhist monk and mathematician Yi Xing created the first water-powered clock. In 868 AD, the first ever book was printed in China.

I had to stop to let that one sink in. The first known book

to have ever been printed. By this point, the tree was already 200 years old, and was probably feeling a bit more nervous when anyone walked past with an axe.

It was genuinely shocking to see how much the population had dropped between 1200 and 1400, as the plague swept across Europe. By the time the apple of another tree had alerted Issac Newton to the existence of gravity, this sequoia had been alive for 1,100 years.

I thought about how small and insignificant we are. About how much we still don't understand. We go about our lives with so much confidence, as if nothing could ever threaten our existence. And yet, it only takes a quick glance at the lifespan of this tree to remind ourselves just how unsteady our situation really is. And how quickly things can change.

I left the museum and did some more sightseeing. I climbed The Monument. I took a walk along Westminster Bridge.

I had the vague notion that this might be in some way inspirational, following, as I would be, in the footsteps of William Wordsworth. As it happened, it was just a bit sad. It had begun to rain quite heavily. Big Ben was completely obscured by scaffolding, mid-renovation, giving everything the grandeur and glamour of a construction site. A lone bagpiper was the only person apart from me to brave the weather, wailing a slow discordant rendition of 'Scotland The Brave' as I passed.

I was sheltering in the entrance of a supermarket, thinking about what exactly I was going to do next, when I started to wonder if it would be possible to go inside the Houses of Parliament.

At the time, this had seemed like a ludicrously ambitious idea. I imagined it would be the kind of thing you'd have to arrange a long time in advance. It would involve many phone calls and complicated forms. It would probably cost a lot of money.

Imagine my surprise, then, when a quick search online revealed that absolutely anyone can go inside the Houses of Parliament, pretty much any time they like.

It doesn't even cost that much.

This might not be in any way surprising to you. Maybe you've already been inside the Houses of Parliament. Maybe you've been loads of times. And by making a big deal out of this, perhaps I'm just revealing how much of a small town, simpleminded peasant I really am.

But to learn that I could go into the actual Houses of Parliament, right that second, for very little money, was truly, properly awe-inspiring. I was gobsmacked. It was like finding out the headquarters of MI5 had been open to the public the whole time, I'd just never bothered to google it.

With nothing else to do, and with the downpour already soaking into my socks, I joined a queue next to a statue of Oliver Cromwell and waited to get inside. I passed through some airport-style security, where my backpack was scanned and I was told that I was not, under any circumstances, allowed to take photographs. After this, you were pretty much free to do whatever you liked.

I remember feeling that, in the current climate, the fact that hordes of the general public were still passing in and out of this building was a little bit iffy. It seemed to me, out of all the places you might want to protect from a new and potentially deadly virus, the very centre of the government would probably be somewhere at the top of that list. Then again, if it was closed that day, I would have had to go to the London Eye instead. And who really wants to do that?

I wandered through dimly lit medieval hallways, passing politicians and journalists as they rushed by. I stood in an empty Westminster Hall, in the same spot Henry the Eighth would once have done.

The weight of history in here was immense. There was an atmosphere of ritual, of continuity. Like how I imagine it feels to join the freemasons.

I went to listen to a debate in the House of Commons. On the way in, two security guards were chatting to each other.

'Did you hear Genesis are reforming?' one said.

'I know – as if things couldn't get any worse.'

I stepped into the viewing gallery with a group of other tourists. We each took a seat on a row of wooden benches. The gallery was separated from the rest of the chamber by a huge wall of bulletproof glass. Below us were the rows of green leather seats, the speaker in his wig and ancient-looking chair, topped with a canopy and covered in carvings. It all felt strangely familiar.

The debate that day was about the steep rise in homes that had been destroyed by flood damage. Looking around the room, I noticed there weren't really many politicians taking part. There were about five MPs on each side.

The secretary for agriculture stood up and said that everything was fine. Then a member of the opposition started to talk about the effects of global warming, saying that the flooding was only going to get worse if we didn't do something about it.

It didn't seem like anybody was really listening. Even the other members of the opposition looked distracted, as they joked around with each other or checked their emails. For the second time that day, I was frightened by humanity's baffling over-confidence.

Meanwhile, Australia had begun a policy of containment and the death toll in Italy had reached the highest number outside China.

A Word with the Whale

Have you ever been inside
the Natural History Museum?
Lucy went on a trip with school,
it was stranger than a dream.
She stepped into that great hall
and could not believe her eyes
when she saw the Blue Whale skeleton
that floated in the sky.

It was bigger than she'd pictured it,
a truly massive scale,
from the girder of its jawbone
to the tree trunk of its tail;
its belly like a block of flats
that filled her heart with awe.
She wondered how they got it in,
it was bigger than the door.

She shouted *Hello*, who knows why,
she didn't think it would reply,
to her surprise the creature moved its head.
It looked around the open space,
then directly at her face.
It answered her, and this is what it said:

I am a whale, a whale am I.
It's clear, no one would disagree,
I am the largest creature that has lived
throughout all history.
I've swum down to the deepest depths
to hunt upon the ocean floor,
I've crossed the planet countless times,
I've glimpsed each distant shore.

But then the land folk came with boats
and spears on the attack,
they took away my family,
they turned my waters black,
my bones are hanging here
for all to see beneath these rafters,
reminding how much can be lost
if we are not looked after.

Then in that moment,
Lucy felt her teacher tap her shoulder,
she'd wandered off, two hours had passed,
the trip was nearly over.
How could time have slipped away?
No one believed her tale,
but she never forgot the story
of the day she met the whale.

18

JAYWICK

IT WAS NOW THE 5TH OF MARCH 2020 and I was sitting at the front of a single-decker bus as it pulled into the last location I would ever visit as a Door-to-Door Poet.

I pressed the bell and thanked the driver, before stepping off into an absolutely massive shower.

The word 'shower' gets overused a lot these days. But this was the force and quantity of an actual shower. Within seconds, I could feel the water seeping through the seams of my jacket. I could barely see a metre in front of my face.

I was standing on a road next to a construction site, peering out through the downpour. I started walking towards the seafront.

The day before this, I'd left the Houses of Parliament and jumped straight on a train to Essex to visit Jaywick. I'd just about managed to squeeze into the packed carriage before the doors shut behind me. As we trundled along, passengers were murmuring about the ever-changing situation. Every time someone coughed, you could feel the space collectively wince. Business people took calls, trying to reassure their clients.

'There's nothing to worry about,' said a man in a grey suit. 'It only affects people with a very specific blood type.'

Clacton-on-Sea was the nearest I could get to Jaywick by rail. It was already late by the time I arrived and I spent a long time wandering around the suburbs looking for somewhere to eat. After much searching, I found a petrol station and bought myself a cheap cheese pastie, before heading over to the Esplanade Hotel.

The Esplanade Hotel was a big old Victorian building, painted dark grey, with palm trees and a fish and chip shop attached to it. There didn't seem to be anywhere I could stay in Jaywick itself, so I'd decided to book myself a room here instead.

When I got inside, two police officers were standing at the reception. A member of staff was giving them the room number of one of the guests.

'You'd better go and check it out,' she said.

The officers nodded and walked solemnly upstairs.

A part of me wanted to ask if everything was OK. But I decided it was probably best not to talk about it. Soon after, the police came back down with a man, who they subsequently took into the bar area for 'a chat'. It wasn't the best first impression.

But everything seemed clean and organised. And the receptionist told me I'd been upgraded to a bigger room with a sea view, on account of a last minute cancellation. It was good news, though I couldn't help wondering if this had something to do with the man being arrested next door.

I woke up the following day and went downstairs for a

complimentary bowl of muesli. There was only one other customer there – a contractor doing some building work nearby. I sat down at a Formica table while, on a TV in the corner, a news reporter was talking about a possible ban on travel.

'We've had tickets booked for Mallorca for ages,' the waitress said, overhearing the announcement. 'I don't care what happens, I'm going.'

Looking back, I don't think any of us really understood how much this was about to disrupt our lives.

I checked the weather forecast while I ate my cereal. It was not good news. There was going to be heavy rain and wind all day. This was not going to help me start a conversation with some strangers.

By this point, the mission was quickly turning into a farce. Here we were, collectively hurtling towards the apocalypse. I was jumping from place to place with barely any time to think about what I was doing. And, as if the threat of an impending biological disaster wasn't enough to put people off answering the door to a poet, I'd now be approaching them in the middle of a storm too.

Even at the time, I could see the funny side.

Maybe this was the logical conclusion to it all, I mused. Whatever happened next, at least I would be going out with a bang.

I put on a bright yellow raincoat and grabbed my briefcase. I stepped out of the hotel and boarded a bus bound for Jaywick.

Jaywick is a small coastal town in the South East. I think

it would be fair to say it's had its share of problems over the years. Once a popular holiday resort, Jaywick has been dubbed the UK's 'Most Deprived Town'.

In a bizarre turn of events, it was also once used as a warning in one of Donald Trump's political campaigns. During a 2018 mid-term election in Illinois, a poster was created by the Republican party. It showed an image of a street in Jaywick, above which was printed the words: 'Only YOU Can Stop This Becoming a REALITY!'

The implication was that if you were to vote for the rival – the lefty Democrat Bill Foster – Illinois would slip into an economic recession so extreme that the entire state would become indistinguishable from the UK town of Jaywick.

As you can probably imagine, the people of Jaywick were a little bit miffed about this.

It serves as an example of how, both nationally and internationally, Jaywick had become shorthand for hard times. There were complaints of a 'dark tourism' industry, people visiting out of nothing more than morbid curiosity, desperate to get a photo in front of a boarded-up shop or a messy street corner.

I wanted to go to Jaywick with an open mind. I wondered if that might change the way I felt about the place. And I was thinking, if I'd visited the most expensive properties in the UK, maybe it was time to get a bit of balance. As well as this, I'd asked people on social media where they thought the project would never work and Jaywick had been one of the suggestions. Challenge accepted, I suppose.

But as I approached the town that day, I couldn't help but

worry that I might already be too late. The idea that people might be too afraid to talk to me because of Covid was now a very real possibility. And the feeling was mutual. I'd started sanitising my hands after knocking on every door. I'd made the decision to avoid going into people's homes at all costs.

It seemed like, if I failed here, it would be reasonable to accept that it was over. That something as eccentric as Door-to-Door Poetry was no longer possible in the current climate. Maybe it never would be possible again. One way or another, I knew this was the end of the line.

With the feeling that I was approaching the final hurdle, I arrived at Jaywick seafront that afternoon. I reached a street called Brooklands. Across the road, there were yellow sand dunes covered in wild grass, the foamy sea crashing against the shore just beyond them.

I'd picked Brooklands because it was very long, which meant there should be lots of people to ask, right? With its premium coastal views, I was also hoping it might bring something of a picturesque quality to my final trip. I'd always wanted to visit the beach as a Door-to-Door Poet.

But as I stood in the storm that day, it wasn't exactly the idyllic view I'd been hoping for. The wind whirled around me in all directions. The rain was now pouring along the road in wide streams, creating ponds in the occasional pot holes. I felt like I was at the centre of Niagara Falls.

From the top of the street, I took a closer look at the houses, a long row of prefab bungalows stretching off into the distance. They were mostly white and pebbledash. Every now and again you spotted a wildcard – one painted bright turquoise with a load of yucca plants outside. Occasionally, you passed one with broken windows, or a missing roof.

If I had to sum up the whole of Jaywick in one word, it would be the word 'bungalow'. It's the first thing you notice when you arrive. It's like a bungalow convention. Bungalow after bungalow after bungalow. Bungalows of all different shapes and sizes. Some of them wide and flat, some of them compact as sheds, some with jagged pointy roofs that look almost Scandinavian. I don't think I saw a single building that wasn't a bungalow the entire time I was there.

I found out later that these bungalows were all built at roughly the same time – in the 1930s. They were made to be holiday homes, although these days they were nearly all used as permanent residences.

I knew I needed to get moving. It wasn't the kind of weather you wanted to be standing around in. The trouble was, Brooklands was much busier than I'd been expecting. A seemingly endless procession of taxis, white vans and buses now came speeding past, all sending out huge waves of water as they raced through the puddles on the road.

An even bigger problem was that I'd realised there was no footpath. There was just the bungalows, then the road, then a concrete wall, which I think was some kind of flood defence. I tried to take a picture of the scene but the rain had filled up inside my camera lens, distorting every image like a funhouse mirror.

Traffic or not, it was time to get on with it. I had four layers on and I was already soaked to the bone.

I ran across the road just as a double-decker bus came

speeding past. It covered me in a tidal wave of water.

At the first pebbledash bungalow there was a 'Beware of the Shih Tzu' sticker on the door. There was no Shih Tzu and no answer.

At the next bungalow, a woman with black hair and glasses came out. She told me she was busy.

At the third bungalow, I couldn't for the life of me find any door at all, so I decided to miss this one out and carry on.

I worked my way along the street. There were a few replies, a few nos. A man in a blue polo-neck told me he had something in the oven. Shortly after, a man with long scraggly hair came out, completely bollock-naked.

'I can see you're busy,' I said. He nodded and quickly closed the door behind him.

Part of what made knocking here so difficult was the sheer logistics of it. The houses were all on the left-hand side of the street, so there was no way of facing the traffic as I went along. This meant that, every minute or so, I'd hear an engine roaring behind me and have to quickly press myself up against a garden wall, as another bus or van came speeding past. Sometimes the road was so waterlogged it resembled a river. Trench foot was becoming a legitimate concern. I was again filled with the fear that I might already be too late.

I kept knocking. There were some more no answers. At one house, a man in a blue hoodie said he would have been interested, only he was just about to go and help out at the community centre. Then, a few doors down, a really tall lad in a baseball cap came out. I asked if he had a minute. For the first time that day, he said yes.

I started to show him my introductory poem.

'I'm a Door-to-Door Poet, and I know that sounds quite crazy—'

He stopped me.

'That's not poetry,' he said, in a tone that sounded highly impressed. 'That's magic!'

I breathed an internal sigh of relief. This was it. Everything was going to be OK. I knew it would work in the end. I just needed to hold on.

Emboldened by the feedback, I carried on with the poem.

'Didn't you hear what I just said!?' he shouted. 'I said I DON'T want no SPELL cast on me, man!!'

At this, he slammed the door and I stepped back, defeated, into the waterlogged road.

I was beginning to come to terms with the likelihood of failure. It seemed wrong – unthinkable even – that it could end like this, on this soggy day in Jaywick. I was so close. I only needed to find two people to reach the finishing line.

But there was no denying it. It just wasn't working. I'd been knocking on doors for over an hour and I wasn't sure how much longer I could physically keep this up. My jaw was rattling, my hands were shaking.

Then I spotted a woman with red hair and tattoos on her arms. She was getting some shopping delivered.

'Excuse me,' I shouted, as the driver passed her the last of the bags. 'I know you're in the middle of something. But I was just wondering, maybe when you're finished?'

I started my poem from out in the road. The driver looked at us both disappointedly before getting in his van and speeding away. But the woman seemed interested. She stood in the doorway, surrounded by carrier bags, listening intently and smiling as I spoke. Halfway through, her next-door neighbour stuck his head out of the window.

'Can you shut up with that fucking poem please? It's annoying my dog.'

I apologised.

I asked the woman if I could stand a bit closer. She said that would be fine.

She told me her name was Sarah. At her front door a few moments later, I thanked Sarah for stopping to talk, especially as she was in the middle of putting the shopping away.

'That's alright,' she said.

I explained what I'd been up to. I asked her what was important to her.

'Well, I moved here from London a few years ago,' she told me. 'It's a very different way of life.'

I asked what made it different.

At this point, her next-door neighbour stuck his head out of the window again.

'I said, could you keep it down? Please!'

I apologised again. In a semi-whisper now, I asked Sarah what made Jaywick so different.

'Well, you say hello about a hundred times a day. We all cook meals for each other. Tonight, I'm making pizza pockets. Also, if someone hasn't seen you in a few days, they'll give you a knock, just to make sure you're OK.'

I asked how that compared with London.

'Oh, it wasn't like that in London at all,' she said. 'I could go weeks without talking to anyone.'

I thought this was really interesting. I asked Sarah why she thought the people here were so sociable. But, at this point, the really tall lad from down the road came walking past. He stopped at the gate behind us.

'Here, Sarah!' he shouted, chest puffed out. 'You don't want to be talking to him, man. He's a magician.'

I tried to assure the lad that I was not a magician. But he was not very happy. Not very happy at all.

'Seriously,' he said. 'Leave her alone.'

At this point, Sarah's next-door neighbour stuck his head out of the window again.

'What's going on?'

'It's this guy, man. He's some fucking magician, knocking on all the doors.'

'He's not a magician,' Sarah explained. 'He's just a poet.'

'Look, if you all don't keep it down, I'm setting the dog on you.'

'Do it, man,' said the tall lad. 'Set the dog on him. Seriously, Sarah, the guy's a fucking wizard.'

With my heart now racing, Sarah and I tried to persuade the tall lad I wasn't a wizard. Then we promised her next-door neighbour we'd be quiet. The tall lad skulked off down the street, and the neighbour retreated back inside, off to console his poor, heavily tormented dog.

'Sorry about that,' Sarah said. 'People get a bit grumpy when you knock on their doors here. We've had a lot of bad publicity.'

I told Sarah I'd read some of the press coverage. She told me it was a regular occurrence.

'Someone came down recently. They just sat on the wall taking pictures of us without our permission. They always come looking for a bad story, but half of what they use isn't even true.'

I asked her if there was anywhere nearby I should visit – anywhere that showed off the good side of Jaywick.

'You should head back along the beach, a little further up. I take the kids there all the time. And there's Ozzy's down the road, too. He does the best fish and chips in the world.'

Feeling like I had enough to go on, I made my goodbyes and made plans for the delivery.

I won't lie – I'd been a little shaken up by her neighbours. But Sarah's hospitality had gone a long way towards putting me back at ease.

And I could empathise here too. Not long before this, Shields Road, a mere fifteen-minute walk from my house, had been voted the 'Ugliest High Street in the Country'. I remember walking down that road the day the news broke. I saw a journalist with a very big camera, taking pictures of some rubbish bins in a nearby alleyway.

It can make you feel angry when a stranger comes to your home looking for the worst bits. It can make you feel a bit more suspicious of strangers, too.

But despite the many obstacles in our way, Sarah had taken the time to get involved, to share her story with me. This meant the absolute world. And as I waved goodbye to her and carried on down the street, the reality of what was happening was starting to give me goosebumps. Sarah was person number twenty-nine. I only had one more to go.

It felt like the tide was turning. It had stopped raining now and a beam of sunlight was bursting through a crack in the cloudy sky. I tried a few more doors. There were a few no answers. Then I got to a house with a bird feeder and a picnic bench outside. I tapped on the door and a woman came out in a multi-coloured jumper with feather earrings.

This was Jacqueline.

'Yeah, I'd be up for that,' she said. 'I used to write a bit of poetry myself.'

It turned out Jacqueline had a big passion for travelling. In fact, her dad was a Romani traveller, and she told me this was a huge part of who she was. She pointed to a van around the corner, a big white Transit with a chequered pattern on the bonnet. She explained that she regularly went off all over the country. Her son was a professional mountain-bike racer, and at the minute she was planning a trip to Fort William, where he was having a race.

But Jacqueline said it was never very long before she was planning her next trip away.

'You know when it's time to move,' she explained. 'You get "the calling". The wind calls you and you just have to go.'

Finding Jacqueline at this particular moment felt important. There seemed to be a lovely synchronicity in the fact that I'd spent a year journeying around the country and was now talking to someone about the nature of travel itself. Jacqueline told me that her upbringing had had a big effect on the way she felt about home.

'I was born on the road,' she said, smiling. 'So I don't have a home town. But, in a way, that means everywhere is my home.'

It felt like the perfect note to end on.

I made plans for the delivery, then said my goodbyes to Jacqueline. I crossed the road and climbed over the flood defence onto the beach. I began to walk across the dunes. It felt unreal – like I was on another planet.

The clouds parted. The next thing I knew, I was standing in a quiet bay, basking in glorious sunshine. Crystal-clear water was lapping gently against the golden sand. It was really peaceful.

Thirty poems. Three-hundred-and-ninety-eight days. I could hardly believe this was happening.

Granted, I still had to actually write something for Sarah and Jacqueline. And there was the small matter of the deliveries. But to have reached this point in Jaywick that afternoon felt like a huge victory.

Turning back towards the town, I knew I couldn't hang about. I would have to go home and get started as soon as possible. But not right now. Right now, I needed to do something very important. Something absolutely vital. I needed to get myself some fish and chips.

On Visiting Jaywick

Yes, Jaywick, I'll confess my reservations.
Your name I'd heard, your headlines I had read.
I took the bus, explained my destination,
the driver fixed me with a look of dread.

But on that evening, walking on your beach,
the sky was clear, the sun bobbed on the waves,
the soft and golden sand was at my feet,
dog walkers smiled and went about their day.

And honestly? It took me by surprise,
your natural beauty shook away my blues,
I couldn't help but pause and wonder why
this scene had never featured on the news.

For certain as each summer fades to brown,
the tabloids yearly come here for a snap
of what they've dubbed a run-down, worthless town
(though who's in charge of it, they never ask).

They hunt for weeds and windows that need fixed,
they hover round like poachers in the road,
but do they stay for views as grand as this
before they pen their articles of woe?

Because I know you have your problems, Jaywick.
But people here are welcoming and kind.
And Ozzy's does the perfect fish and chips,
next to a pub that's called *Never Say Die*.

But that won't make the front page, nor the sea
as it glitters here above your coastal shelf,
when papers only deal in misery,
I'm pleased I found the truth out for myself.

19

THE END OF THE ROAD

I ONCE READ A VERY GOOD BOOK about the plague.

That's not the best conversation starter, is it? As an opening statement, it's not exactly the kind of thing that would go down well at a children's birthday party, or during an acceptance speech.

But poets can be quite a morbid bunch sometimes, you know. I've walked in many a graveyard for fun in my time. All I can do is ask you to stick with me, as we take a brief diversion into the macabre.

I'll say it again, as if it really needed repeating: I once read a very good book about the plague.

It's called *A Journal of the Plague Year* by Daniel Defoe. I read it after my Door-to-Door Poetry adventure was over. It's about the last breakout of the plague in London, in 1665. It's based on a true story. If nothing else, it reminded me that history has a nasty habit of repeating itself.

One of the things that really stood out was the way the news first reached England. Before the plague spread here, there were reports of an outbreak in Holland, which had been very 'violent', especially in Amsterdam. Then, in words that sounded spookily familiar by the time I read them, the narrator tells us that the government knew exactly what was coming. That they'd already: 'had a true Account of it, and several Counsels were held about Ways to prevent its coming over; but it was all kept very private. Hence it was, that this Rumour died off again, and People began to forget it, as a thing we were very little concern'd in, and that we hoped was not true.'

Never had a sentence from the past seemed more applicable to my own life.

But in the 21st century, as much as in the 17th, there had to come a point when those rumours were no longer possible to ignore. And by mid-March in 2020, we were just about reaching that point.

Italy and Spain were now both in lockdown. There was talk of it happening here by the end of the week.

Yet, in spite of this, everyone seemed to be carrying on as normal. People kept going to work, they kept going to restaurants, they kept visiting galleries and playing five-a-side matches. And, on the 16th of March, ten days after I'd first gone to Jaywick, I boarded a train and set off to deliver the final two poems, for Sarah and Jacqueline.

To account for the quickly changing situation, I'd been working to get these poems finished a bit quicker than normal. This had resulted in a lot of late nights, facilitated by a lot of caffeinated beverages. Abnormally large bags were hanging under my eyes. My hands had reached a permanent state of shaking.

I still hadn't had time to figure out what I was going to

do once the project was over. I was again becoming aware of just how much this whole saga was consuming the rest of my life. And when I spoke to Rose about what I was planning, she just sounded really worried.

'You're going to be careful, aren't you?'

I promised her I would.

But even now, in the middle of all this rush and anxiety, it still felt exciting to be this close to the end. It was the final countdown. Yes, it was going to be tight. Yes, there was no margin for error. But I reckoned there was just enough time. I was sure I could get this wrapped up before everything went sideways. I was a man on a mission.

So this was the plan: I was going to get the train down to Clacton-on-Sea and check into the Esplanade Hotel. Then I was going to take the bus over to Jaywick and deliver Jacqueline's poem. Sarah couldn't meet me till the next day, so I was going to spend the night in the Esplanade Hotel, then drop off Sarah's poem, then head back to Newcastle.

On the way to the station, my friend Robin phoned me. He teaches in a primary school in Shenzhen in the south of China. When the pandemic started there, he was on holiday in Thailand. Since then, he'd been jumping from country to country, desperately trying to find a place that wasn't going into a lockdown, seemingly unwilling or unable to accept what life might be like after that.

Looking back now, I think we were both coping in very similar ways.

Robin told me he was currently in Bali. Like lots of other places, the restrictions were starting to kick in and he was beginning to run out of options.

He flew back to Shenzhen that afternoon. He was greeted at the airport by an army of government officials in hazmat suits. They lined the passengers up against a wall, before spraying them down with disinfectant. We found out later that Robin had been on the last plane allowed back into China, before the country completely closed its borders.

Meanwhile, on the other side of the world, I was on a train to Clacton-on-Sea, and the only thing I could think about was successfully delivering these poems.

It may seem a little silly, considering the cataclysmic events that were now unfolding. I suppose any right-minded person would have probably posted the poems and forgotten all about it. Maybe I should have.

But, no matter how hard I tried, there was a stubbornness in me that I just couldn't shake. I was *supposed* to go back and deliver every poem by hand, to read them out for each person on the doorstep. This was the way it had always worked before. It's what I'd been doing since I first started this journey.

I think a part of me just couldn't let go of that. I had become, in many ways, obsessed. Unhealthily so, really. Every fibre of my being was fixated on ending this big stupid adventure in exactly the way I'd first planned it, global pandemic or not.

The train down to Essex seemed a little quieter than usual. When I got off at Clacton station, it seemed quieter here too. At the Esplanade Hotel, the receptionist greeted me energetically before going on to talk a lot about the complimentary breakfast. And when I say a lot, I mean a lot.

'It'll still be on,' she stuttered. 'We think. We're not really sure at the minute.'

I couldn't understand what all the fuss was about.

I went up to my room and put down my bags. I checked my phone.

It was at this point that I realised I was already too late.

Boris Johnson had just given a speech. He was advising people to stay indoors and only travel for work or essential food and medicine. There was an uncharacteristically sombre expression on his face. The reporters kept using the word 'unprecedented'.

The moments that followed seemed to take place outside of my body. It was as if I was an insect, watching it all unfold from a corner of the dusty hotel ceiling.

I paced backwards and forwards on the tiny patch of worn carpet at the foot of the bed. I tried to get my head around it.

It wasn't supposed to be like this. I was supposed to have till the end of the week. What was I going to do?

In the space of a few minutes, the whole world had become incredibly threating. I thought about Rose, about how I was ever going to get back home. The space between the hotel and my house now felt galactic. A seething mass of frightening, shadowy creatures. An endless sprawl of buildings filled with sinister and unknowable horrors.

I tried to catch my breath.

I was here. There was nothing I could do to change that. But what to do next?

I found myself scrolling through pages of government

guidance. This just seemed to raise more questions than it really answered. I wished there was some kind of a helpline I could ring. But there wasn't. Like everyone else, I was left to figure it out on my own.

It was all a bit confusing. On the one hand, Johnson was calling for an end to all 'non-essential contact' and 'unnecessary travel'. He'd asked people to start working from home, 'where they possibly can', and avoid pubs, clubs and theatres.

On the other hand, the pubs, clubs and theatres were going to stay open, along with restaurants, schools, cinemas, and pretty much every other public building in the country.

My thoughts turned to the mission at hand.

Was it right to carry on? I mean, this was technically work. Hundreds of thousands of people were going to carry on travelling to and from their jobs as normal. Maybe I could keep going too?

It felt like it all depended on how much the people on the doorstep wanted their poems delivered. I got in touch with Sarah and Jacqueline and asked them if they still thought I should come. It was a resounding yes.

Later that day, I took the bus over to Jaywick. I walked down Brooklands and reached Jacqueline's house. I was about to knock on her door when it opened, as if by magic. We both jumped.

'Oh,' she said. 'I was just about to get something from the van. Come on, we can sit in there.'

Without really thinking, I said OK.

We climbed inside the camper van. It had everything you

could need in there. A little sink and drying rack, a hob. The walls were decorated with multi-coloured mandalas and throws.

Jacqueline perched on the bed, and I found a spot on a wooden stool nearby. I read her my poem. Then we started to talk about everything that was unfolding.

Jacqueline was the first person I spoke to after the news had broken. I'll never forget her expression that day, the uncertainty in her voice.

'It's scary,' she said. 'You read about something in the papers and then, all of a sudden, it's on your doorstep.'

When I first met her, Jacqueline had seemed like such a relaxed and confident soul. Seeing how nervous she was about all this made me realise how serious it was.

An awkward silence followed. I didn't really know what to say. I wanted to fill the space with something so, without giving it much thought, I asked if the trip to Fort William was still going ahead.

'Definitely,' she said, before pausing. 'We might just have to put it off till May, or June. Although…they're saying it might go on for a bit longer than that now.'

It was clear that neither of us really knew what was going to happen next. I opened the door of the van and started to make my goodbyes.

Even in this moment, despite all the worry, all the confusion, I still felt grateful to have had the chance to see Jacqueline one last time. To have delivered her poem in person, to have seen her smile when I read it out.

'I'll send you some photos from Scotland,' she said, as I

stepped out of the van.

I told her I'd look forward to it.

I waved goodbye to Jacqueline and thanked her for getting involved. Knowing how close I was to the end, it meant more to me now than it ever really had before.

Setting Off

Jacqueline, you're getting the van ready,
packing your bags.
Who knows where, or how long you'll be?

Your dad, he was Romani.
This stuff is in the blood, you tell me.
The wind gives you a sign.

Jacqueline, your earrings are feathers
and your eyes are wise.
You know your house is always temporary.

You stop at any forest
or field that takes your fancy,
drinking in the peacefulness of anonymity.

Jacqueline, I wish you
smooth tarmac, starry skies,
welcoming smiles.

Jacqueline, I wish you
strange new foods, waterproof ceilings
and great heights.

You told me you're unrooted,
there is no return address,
from childhood all that's certain is the road.

But like the wind you follow,
there's no nations, there's no borders,
and any patch of earth can be your home.

20

THE FINAL DOOR

BEFORE I TELL YOU THE END of this story, I need to be honest about something. A lot has gone on since that last delivery in Jaywick. I wish I could have known then what I know now. But I didn't.

It's strange to look back on all of this. When I think about my actions, it's clear that I just didn't understand how serious things were getting. We were on the cusp of a big catastrophe. The possibility of catching and spreading Covid was becoming ever more likely. And with the benefit of hindsight, it's easy to see that carrying on in Jaywick was morally dubious, at best.

I can see now that I shouldn't have ever boarded that train to Clacton-on-Sea. I shouldn't have gone to Jaywick to deliver Jacqueline's poem. And I shouldn't have stayed in Essex to meet Sarah the next day.

But the past, we're told, is a different country. And it's important to remember that, at the time, no one really knew what they were supposed to be doing. There was no guidance about masks or leaving the house. There was no social distancing policy.

Immediately after Johnson's speech, people began panic-buying all kinds of products. Supermarket shelves up and down the country were stripped bare. Customers started brawling in queues, ripping the last items from other people's trolleys. For a brief moment, it felt like society was teetering on the edge of a complete breakdown.

But even that doesn't really explain my thinking at the time. Because the truth is, even then, I was beginning to have my doubts about staying in Jaywick.

After I dropped off Jacqueline's poem, I went for a worried vegetable dhansak in a deserted restaurant near the Esplanade Hotel. Much like Jacqueline herself, the staff had seemed surprised to see me. I was beginning to feel like some kind of a fugitive.

As I half-heartedly nibbled on a poppadom, I started to wonder if I'd made a bit of a mistake.

Sure, I wasn't technically breaking any laws. Door-to-Door Poetry was work, or at least something you'd vaguely describe as work. According to the government's new guidance, I was well within my rights to carry on doing it.

But as the minutes passed I was beginning to wonder if that was really the point. In amongst the chaos, I couldn't help but notice the way the project was shifting. This adventure had begun with a simple question: *Could I do this? Would anyone stop to talk?* Now that question was changing into a very different one.

I woke up in the Esplanade Hotel the next day. I pulled the covers from my face and dragged myself out of bed. I had not slept well.

My phone had been buzzing all night with a dizzying flood of messages. Breaking headlines. Questions from family and friends. Everything was moving really fast.

In spite of the government's advice, a lot of cinemas and theatres had started to close. Despite legally being allowed to stay open, they didn't feel they could justify it any more. And they weren't the only ones either. Most people I knew were now working from home. When I told them where I was and what I was doing, the general response was disbelief.

When I rang Rose and explained that I was going to stay in Essex for an extra day, she didn't sound angry – just really disappointed.

'I guess you'll have to live with the consequences of that,' she said.

Deep down, I knew what I was doing was wrong.

Maybe I was in shock. Maybe I was just being selfish. Whatever the reason, I couldn't do it. I couldn't turn around. After all this time, I couldn't entertain the idea of not finishing this, of walking away without delivering Sarah's poem.

I sat down on a pink armchair in the hotel room. I opened the curtains. The sun was rising over a still blue sea, the palm trees around the building blowing in the breeze. I made a cup of tea and tried to pull myself together. I started to come up with a plan.

It turned out the Royal Mail were still delivering letters. When it came to packages, they were leaving them on the doorstep, then standing two metres back. It felt like this might be the right way forward.

On the one hand, I don't think anyone could argue that

dropping off Sarah's poem was what Johnson was really alluding to when he'd talked about 'essential contact'. It wasn't like I was delivering a medicine, or performing CPR.

But it struck me that, on this very same day, Sarah could have ordered a new set of garden chairs, or a copy of *Cool Runnings* on DVD. And this would have subsequently been delivered to her house in very much the same way that my poem would be delivered as well.

Was my poetry more or less important than *Cool Runnings*? It was a thorny issue, and one I still don't really know the answer to. But so long as this was something that Sarah wanted, it felt like I could justify going to visit her.

However, if I was going to see her that day, I would need to print out a finished copy of her poem first. Ordinarily, I would have printed this out before I left home. But I'd been so busy that I'd only managed to finish Sarah's poem on the train journey down to Jaywick. I'd considered giving her a handwritten version instead. But if you ever have the misfortune of trying to decipher my handwriting, you'll understand why that wasn't really an option.

Instead, I packed up my stuff and set off down the road to Clacton Library.

As I stepped through the automatic doors, I was shocked to see how busy it was. The main room was packed with people, all in varying states of panic.

Everyone was talking about the news. Some were saying the measures were right, others that they weren't.

'I bet you're pleased you voted for him now,' a man with an Elvis quiff remarked, to no one in particular.

'You can't just give up on life,' a woman of pensionable age kept exclaiming, over and over again.

Everyone seemed to be talking to themselves, all at once and at great volume. It was like sitting backstage in a room full of Shakespearean actors, all rehearsing different monologues at the same time.

The staff had built a makeshift barricade in front of their desk out of No Entry rope and chairs. While I was sitting at a computer a few minutes later, a lady came in and gingerly walked over to it.

'Excuse me, do you know if I'll still be doing the children's story time?' she asked.

At this, the librarian shrugged and shook her head, in a way that suggested her guess was as good as anyone's.

Armed with the printed poem, I left the library and took the bus over to Jaywick. On the way, I passed a sign for a crazy golf course, no doubt certifiably sane in the current climate. We drove through hilly green countryside. The weather was calm and sunny. I felt tired and scared.

I got off the bus and walked towards the coast. At the seafront, I stopped to take a picture of a now-deserted beach, the waves crashing solemnly against the sand. I headed down Brooklands till I reached Sarah's door.

I walked up the front path and took a deep breath. I rang the bell. I paused and listened for what felt like minutes.

After a while, I realised I was still holding my breath. I made a conscious effort to exhale, but in a way that would direct the air to the side, instead of straight forwards.

It had been a lot longer than a minute now. I tried the

bell again. After a minute more, it was clear there was no one home.

On any normal day I would have tried again. I would have texted or called Sarah to see if there was a better time to come back. But I knew that wasn't an option here. Not now. I'd already stayed in Jaywick much longer than I really should have.

And there was always the possibility that Sarah's absence wasn't entirely accidental, either. What if she'd changed her mind? Everything had been moving so fast. Public opinion was shifting by the second. Sarah had probably been thinking very similar things to me in the past twenty-four hours.

What if she didn't feel comfortable about this any more? What if she didn't want me to come and visit her, but she couldn't find the words to say it?

It didn't feel right to put any more pressure on her. Not with the way things were going. I could see now what I needed to do next.

I lifted the printed poem out of my briefcase. I held it in my hands for a moment, the weight of the paper resting against my fingertips. It felt thick and loaded with unintended meaning. I wondered how Sarah would feel about its arrival.

This wasn't how I'd pictured it. I couldn't believe this was really the end. But I understood now that it had to be. I pushed the last ever Door-to-Door Poetry poem through Sarah's letterbox. Then I let go of it, listening as it fell and landed on the floor of her hallway.

The train back to Newcastle was completely empty. It felt

like I'd found some kind of an ending. As I changed at King's Cross, I stopped to buy the last few cans of beer I could find in a desolate-looking supermarket. Rose called to say that her school, along with every other school in the country, was closing, as of tomorrow. We were entering something that looked a lot more like a lockdown.

I boarded my final train home. As we pulled out of London, I gazed through the window. I began to take hundreds of pictures, one after the other, almost without thinking. They were pictures of completely ordinary things: riversides, pylons, cooling towers.

It felt like this might be the last train journey I took for a very long time. Though it's embarrassing to admit it now, it felt like it might be the last train journey I ever took in my life.

I got off at a deserted Newcastle station. As I stepped onto the white marble floor, it began to fully sink in for the first time: it was over. There was nothing left to do. As I got closer to the exit, I found myself slowing down, my steps becoming heavier and less certain.

For the past few days, I'd been living in a bubble of my own creation. I'd been so busy working towards this final delivery there had been no time to think about anything else. In doing this, I'd insulated myself from some of the most scary thoughts that came with what was now happening in the world at large. Ideas about what this might mean for me and the people I cared about most. But that bubble was now starting to burst. And the time had come to face up to what was really going on here. To accept this ending for what it actually was.

From this point forward, I would no longer be a Door-to-Door Poet. I would no longer have a mission to keep myself occupied, or to give me a sense of purpose. On a practical level, I would also no longer have a job, or any kind of financial security. There were a lot of things to think about. A lot of things I didn't know the answer to.

I found myself standing at the ticket barriers a few minutes later, unable to walk through them.

I just couldn't. No matter how hard I tried. It was as if I was frozen. Every time I tried to take a step, my legs would seize up, my subconscious refusing to allow the movement.

For one reason or another, my mind had decided this was the line. This was the boundary – the customs office between the before and the after. On this side of the barriers stood the project and everything I had come to know until now. On the other side stood something else, but I wasn't quite sure what that was yet.

I knew, when I passed through those barriers, everything was going to change. It would probably never change back. I knew when I passed through them, I was stepping out into a very uncertain world.

Last Days

I was leaving King's Cross
when everything locked.
The carriage empty,
the conductor suspiciously upbeat.
We have a lot of free seats today,
spread yourself out and relax,
while, beyond the glass,
fist-fighting over toilet paper.

We picked up speed,
shot into the country.
It occurred to me
this could be the last train I ever take.
Silly.
But I began to make a mental note
of golden fields, patchwork hedgerows,
cooling towers, riversides,
flashing up for a moment before
fading indefinitely.

Maybe, I thought,
my children will ask me
what it felt like to ride on a train.
And I will have to explain
I was mostly looking backwards,
or somewhere into space.

That I never really stopped
to clock what it was,
till it seemed about to vanish
on the very last day.

21

RETURNING

A LOT OF TIME HAS PASSED since that final trip home. I could fill another book with the story of what happened to me. Maybe one day I'll be able to tell you all about it.

For now, I should probably finish this story. And to do that, we're going to need to jump forwards a bit. So with this in mind I'm going to gently pick you up and carry you to the 28th of April 2022, where this whole saga reaches its concluding scenes.

The then Prince Charles had been saying that cows are burping too much. I was sitting in an Indian street-food restaurant in an indoor market in Newcastle, trying not to do the same.

I was with a man called James.

James had very kindly offered to buy me something as a way of saying thanks. Having already been informed that there was no vegetable dhansak, I'd begrudgingly opted for the chana chaat instead.

To be fair, it was fine and rich and had a good kick. When it came down to it, it was nice to have a bit of a change. It's good to break out of your routines every now and again, isn't it?

James had got in touch because he was about to do an art project near my house. He was planning to talk to some people on their doorsteps and record their stories. He was then going to turn these recordings into a podcast. He wanted to ask for a bit of advice.

Somewhat predictably, the conversation had turned to my travels as a Door-to-Door Poet.

'So, Rowan,' James asked, between mouthfuls of curry. 'Where are you going to go next?'

I wasn't really sure what to say.

James seemed genuinely curious. His eyebrows were raised expectantly. He looked poised and ready to hear about the amazing adventure I was surely in the middle of planning.

I wanted to give him an exciting answer, but I didn't know how. An awkward silence followed. Partly because I was trying to think of a way to reply. But partly because I had a chickpea stuck to the roof of my mouth and I was secretly trying to dislodge it with my tongue, which made the silence last even longer than it really needed to.

After what I was hoping he would assume was a very deliberate pause, I told James the answer. I told him the truth – anything more interesting having failed to spring to mind.

'I'm not going anywhere,' I admitted. 'I'm not doing Door-to-Door Poetry any more.'

He seemed a little disappointed.

'Maybe you haven't thought of the right place to visit yet,' he suggested.

I told him I wasn't so sure.

It was a question that was beginning to sound quite familiar. A few weeks before this, I'd been invited to a gathering for artists who like to work 'collaboratively'. I didn't really know what that meant, but it turns out it involves things like being a Door-to-Door Poet.

The event took place in a bar called the Old Coal Yard. It consisted of a series of speeches, followed by some moderate-to-heavy drinking.

I met a lot of interesting people that day. They all seemed really passionate about talking to strangers. Having spent so much time doing this kind of thing on my own, it was nice to get to know some like-minded individuals.

After the presentation, we all sat around in the pub and put the world to rights. We talked, and laughed, and came up with all kinds of ideas. It seemed like whoever I spoke to wanted to ask the same question.

'What's the plan, Rowan? Where are you going to go knocking next?'

Of course, for two years before this, Door-to-Door Poetry hadn't really seemed possible. It just didn't feel right in the circumstances.

Not that this had stopped people connecting with strangers in other ways.

In fact, during the pandemic, people had come up with all kinds of new and kooky ways to meet their fellow citizens. All over the world, they played music from rooftops, they hosted bingo in cul-de-sacs.

One of my favourite things to have stumbled on during the lockdowns was a video of a whole tower block dancing at once. On the same night every week, the residents had arranged to open their curtains at exactly the same time, to fire up some disco lights and lasers and dance in their windows together.

It didn't matter if they couldn't dance very well. It didn't even matter that they couldn't watch each other dancing, and the only people who could see them were passers-by in the street. What mattered was that they were sharing a moment.

But as the pubs and cinemas and theatres started to open up again, the prospect of knocking on doors and writing poems for strangers was once more seeming like a possibility.

And yet, even if it was something I could now feasibly do again, my curiosity appeared to have been satisfied.

I gave every person who asked the same answer. I told them that Door-to-Door Poetry was finished. It had ended on that beach in Jaywick, the day I posted Sarah's poem through her letterbox.

That's not to say I didn't have a whale of a time while I was doing it. Being a Door-to-Door Poet was one of the most exciting things I've ever tried. Whether it was knocking for the first time near my street, or visiting places like Manchester or Grantchester, Boston or Lundy, from some of the busiest to some of the quietest areas in the country. Or my trip to Limerick, or to provisions like St Gemma's and the Syrian families of Kent. I was amazed by the responses I got. The honesty, friendliness and generosity of the people I spoke to genuinely filled me with a faith in humanity that I will never forget.

I also learned a lot. I learned a lot about geography, for starters. And it was interesting to see what happened when, for a whole year, I tried to put aside my fears. To keep an open mind.

Having all of these interactions, it made me think about our relationship with strangers too. It helped me to see that when we make an effort to talk to someone new, someone who lives their life differently to us, we often discover a lot about ourselves in the process. This still feels as important to me now as it did back then.

But there wasn't anywhere else I wanted to go. For me, the conversations I'd had and the places I'd visited were enough.

After resigning from my post as a Door-to-Door Poet, I'd been enjoying settling back into my home town. I'd remembered why I love living in the place I do. All of the big, eccentric characters you come across on any normal day in Newcastle.

Not far from my street lives a man called Mr Funky, a man whose claim to fame is that, in the '80s, he was the North-East's answer to the celebrity fitness guru, Mr Motivator. He has the news clippings to prove it.

As I went about my day, I noticed myself making more of an effort to talk to people. I'd stop to chat to shopkeepers, to fellow passengers on the bus. I liked finding out about them, about what was going on in their lives.

Things in my own life had been changing too. I'd managed to patch up the somewhat gaping holes in my family relationships. I'd managed to find more of what you might call a 'work-life balance'. And even though I still wasn't really sure what I was supposed to be doing, I'd been able to find some rewarding ways to fill my time.

I'd got a job as a community librarian. I'd started running a pop-up library in a local food kitchen in South Tyneside, not far from where I grew up.

There'd been some changes at home, too. Rose had forgiven me for the many months I'd spent ignoring her. In fact, so successful were my efforts to repair the damage, I'd managed to persuade her to marry me. We'd moved into a bigger flat, not far from the one we lived in. We were starting to think of ways we might fill the extra rooms.

And yes, I still thought about Door-to-Door Poetry. Especially when I heard from some of the people I met on my adventures. A year after I dropped off her poem, Jacqueline sent me a message to tell me how she was doing. She told me she'd moved to a commune with a group of other Romani travellers. She was enjoying growing her own vegetables.

I got a message from Wislawa in Boston, too. She posted me some paints you can use to decorate a traditional Polish Easter egg.

I felt (and still feel) incredibly grateful to all the people who stopped to help me on my travels. To all the other people I haven't mentioned in this book. The time we shared meant so much. I believe it has made me a more understanding and more fully formed human being.

But by 2022, my life, it seemed, had shifted gears. The moment had come and gone. And so I told people, no, as much as I'd enjoyed the adventure, it was over. There was simply nowhere else on my list of places to visit. The project was done. Finito. It was time to hang up my briefcase, to file away my business cards. The position of Door-to-Door Poet was now officially vacant.

Some things, I reasoned, were just more important.

Homecoming

So many times
I have called you
from stations
and strange rooms,
between train tracks,
from the backs
of empty cafés.

And I know
I've sounded far away,
as if my dreams
or reasons
could not have flown
further from your side.

But believe me
when I tell you,
I've been grasping
your warmth and light.
I've held on to it
in uncertain streets,
I've cherished it
in far-flung climes.

Even in these times,
it's your love that's been

guiding me through
frightened
nights alone.
It's your kindness
that has lifted me
and carried me back home.

THANK YOU

I would like to give a very special thank you to the following people. Without them this book would not have been possible: everyone who answered the door, whether you agreed to take part or not, Rose, my mam, Stephen, my grandparents, Lisa at Butterflies and Bugs, Julie at Fenside Community Centre, Anna, Daniel Mitchelson, Reece Williams, Bee, for the good times, Hayley and Alan, James, Helen, Kai and Alice for the spare room, Gina Sherman, all the staff on Lundy Island, Dominic Taylor at the Limerick Writers' Centre, Ben Dickenson, Azim and Chantel at St Basil's, Clare, Heather and Amanda at St Gemma's Hospice, Jitka and Dan and all of the staff at Migrant Help, Eklas, Wajid Hussain, Imam Kola, Toby, Kirsten Luckins, Peader Kirk, who directed a show about the project and who taught me what the words 'narrative arc' mean, Kate Fox, who's been a frequent and outstanding mentor, Matt Miller, for reading through my poems at short notice, John Osborne, Will Atkinson and Ben Aitken, for helping me turn the first draft into something much greater than I could have imagined,

Dan Hiscocks at Eye Books and every other person who got in touch to suggest places, to encourage me, or just to tell me they liked the idea.

This journey and the resulting poems were funded by Arts Council England, Apples and Snakes, Migrant Help, ARC Stockton and Northern Stage.

The poem 'Christmas in Hebburn' was originally commissioned by the Royal Voluntary Service. 'Last Days' was commissioned by the National Trust and was first published in *Hopeless Romantic* (National Trust, 2022)

If you have enjoyed *The Door-to-Door Poet*, do please help us spread the word – by putting a review online; by posting something on social media; or in the old-fashioned way by simply telling your friends or family about it.

Book publishing is a very competitive business these days, in a saturated market, and small independent publishers such as ourselves are often crowded out by the big houses. Support from readers like you can make all the difference to a book's success.

Many thanks.
Dan Hiscocks
Founder, Eye Books